Richard Blome

An essay to heraldry in two parts

The first containing the body of heraldry

Richard Blome

An essay to heraldry in two parts
The first containing the body of heraldry
ISBN/EAN: 9783337196752

Printed in Europe, USA, Canada, Australia, Japan

Cover: Foto ©Andreas Hilbeck / pixelio.de

More available books at **www.hansebooks.com**

AN ESSAY TO HERALDRY

In Two Parts.

The *Firſt* Containing (in a Conciſe but Methodical Method, by Rules and Explanations of Bearings) the Body of *Heraldry* :

The *Second*, *Honour* Civil and Military; Being a Treatiſe of the *Nobility* and *Gentry* of *ENGLAND*, as to their *Priviledges*, *Dignities*, &c. According to the Laws and Cuſtoms of our *Realm*.

The whole Illuſtrated with variety of Apt and Proper *Sculptures*, for the better Explanation thereof.

LONDON,

Printed by *T. B.* for *Rich. Blome*, and Sold by him at his Lodgings at *Mr. Conines* next the hanging *Sword* in *Saliſbury Court*, 1684.

TO THE
RIGHT HONOURABLE
GEORGE

Earl of *Berkeley*, Viscount *Du-reſley*, Lord *Berkeley*, *Mawbray*, *Se-grave* and *Bruce*, and Baron of *Ber-keley* Caſtle, *&c.*

My Lord,

THIS *Treatiſe of He-raldry, though ſmall in bulk, yet large in ſub-ſtance comprehending all the cheif and neceſſary Rules in the ſaid Art, which (with no ſmall labour and pains) are digeſted in a methodical method (in way of an Ordinary) in ſeveral Shields engraven on Cop-per Plates ; and for the Explana-*

A 2

tion

tion thereof the ſeveral Coats in each Shield are Blazoned with the names of the Bearers, except to thoſe that are made uſe of only for Examples ; and the number of the Figures refers to the Coat in the Shield, which is reckoned from the firſt in the Dexter cheif. And under the ſaid Heads, Coats of like Bearings may be compriſed, whether of themſelves, or between, or charged upon any of the Honourable Ordinaries ; for it can't be expected that this ſmall Tract ſhould give Examples of all Bearings this being only deſigned for a ſmall Pocket Book, and only to give the Rules with Examples of Bearings, to teach the way of Blazoning any Coat Armour.

The

Epiſtle Dedicatory.

The ſecond Part is a Treatiſe of the Nobility *and* Gentry *of* Eng-land *as to their* Priviledges, Dig-nities, *&c. And for Examples of Bearings I have inſerted* Atchieve-ments *of each* Degree *compleat, that is, with all the external orna-ments as* Mantle, Helmet, Creſt, Motto, *and* Supporters, *hav-ing given your* Honour's Atchieve-ment *for the Example of an* Earl.

My Lord, as on the one hand, I may preſume to ſay that there hath been no-thing yet extant of this nature ſo full in ſo ſmall a Compaſs ; ſo on the other it is my ambition to take this opportu-nity to expreſs the great eſteem I have for your Honour, *as well in reſpect of the nobleneſs of your* Family

which

A 3

which renders you a person interessed in this work, as to testifie my gratitude for your favours showred upon me for the promoting some former undertakings, being indeed a great favourer of all ingenuous Arts, and in particular to HERALDRY *the Subject of this Book. My Lord, your generous Spirit hath ever aimed at a publick Good, many admire you, and most love and honour you.* You are generally beloved for your generous and noble Actions, for your generous and noble Inclinations, and for your generous and noble Principles so that I cannot but receive Commendations for selecting you to the Patronage of this Work. My Lord, if you pardon this my

ambition

ambition I have my ſatisfaction, and can be no better contented than in that and in being ſtiled

My Lord,

Your honours moſt
humble Servant

RICHARD BLOME.

The

THE

AN ESSAY TO HERALDRY.

CHAP. I.

This Chapter treateth of the original & universality, the sundry Denominations, and the original Discipline of Arms and Ensigns, with their use and necessity: Their Sympathy with the Bearers, and conformity with Names, their Definition, Blazon, Distribution, Accidents and Parts, and lastly their Abatements and Rewards of Honour.

THE Dignity and Estimation of *Arms* cannot but be great, if we alone consider that it delights the Beholders, greatly Graces the places where they are erected,

&ted, and gives occasion to the Beholders to make inquiry whose they are, and of what family the bearer is descended.

Before I proceed further, it will not be unnecessary briefly to begin with some *Observations* suitable to this subject, and first, of those *Marks* or *Ensigns* called *Arms*, in Latin *Arma.*

The word *Arma* as in *Guillims Heraldry*, is taken for very natural Instruments, and in this sence Doctor *Casius* doth use the same where he saith, *Arma belluis natura dedit, ut Leoni Dentes, serpenti aculeum,* &c.

It is also taken for all manner of *Instruments* that belong to *Mechanical Trades.*

Instruments Military.
It is likewise taken for all sorts of *Warlike instruments* : But the word *Arma* doth not here signify any of these things, but is taken for *Shields, Targets, Millitary Cassocks, Banners,* and other *Martial Instruments* on which they were *Engraven, Embossed or depicted,* and these were peculiar only to *Martial Men,* and professed *Souldiers,* which to this day is called *Arms,* from the Latin word *Arma.* And *Claudius Fauches* saith that *Armes* have

their

HERALDRY.

their denomination, becaufe *Military Men* did bear their feveral *Devices* as a-forefaid upon their *Shields*.

Guillim faith that *Arms* were called *Symbola*, which fignifies tokens or Marks, which in the time of Hoftility or civil Tumults were given to *Souldiers* by their *Captains* or Chief *Commanders*, for diftin-guifhing of particular Perfons, as well amongft themfelves as from their Ene-mies.

Thefe *Armorial Notes* fo much in re-queft now amongft us, are oft times cal-led *Enfigns*, which comprizeth in gene-ral all *Marks* and *Tokens* of *Honour* due to meritorious Perfons, as well in refpect of their *Government*, *Learning*, *wifdom*, *Magnanimity*, &c. as for their Martial Prowes. Amongft thefe *Enfigns* are thofe *Marks* and *Shapes* of *Animals*, that *Martial Men* ufed to adorn their *Helmets* withal, to the end that they might ap-pear more eminent in the *Field*, and be the better taken notice of for their valo-rous Actions, when they encountred their enemies in Battle, or fhould draw on their forces to fight.

Note the ufe of thefe Enfigns was yet further extended then the Adorning of

Shields

Shields and *Helmets*; for Ships were beautifyed with *Arms* on their *Sterns*, to distinguish the one from the other, as the Ship where St. *Paul* went, whose Badg was *Castor* and *Pollux*; also the fore-Deck of *Europa* that was carried away, had the form of a *Bull* depicted thereon, which gave occasion to the fable, that a *Bull* had stolen away *Europa*, nor did the Antients only use it, but it hath been a Custom in all succeeding Ages, even to this day, and from thence doth come the names of *Ships*.

Definition of *Arms*.

  Arms then, according to original use, are Tokens or Resemblances signifying some Act or Quality of the Bearer, either by some worthy exploit performed in *Military Affairs* (especially if bestowed by a Noble Prince) or else by their Learning and Wisdom, which they do by spending their Spirits in continual study to make themselves fit for the *Patronage* and defence of their Country.

Rebusses.

  Sometimes there are *Arms* born, which may seem to have been devised (in their first *Institution*)according to the Sir-Name of the Bearer, as 3 Castles for *Castleton*; three Gates for *Yates*; three Coneys for
Conisby

Conisby and the like, and such Bearings are called *Rebuffes* being very Antient.

If there were two diſtinct *Families* of one Sir-Name, yet bearing ſeveral *Coat Armors*, it is not evident that they were both extracted from one *Anceſtor*, for the *Coat-Armour* is the expreſs ſign of Diſtinction.

As ſuppoſe there are two Families divers in Name, and iſſued from ſeveral *Parents*, and both of them do bear one *Coat Armour*, and the name of one of them is agreeable to the *Coat Armour*, and the other diſſonant from the ſame; now the queſtion is, to which doth this *Coat* belong; in anſwer it may according to probability be conjectured, to belong to him whoſe appellation is agreeable therewith, rather than to the other. And it is obſervable, that two diſtinct *Families* ought not, nor are they allowed to bear one and the ſame *Coat-Armour*, but amongſt the *Welſh* this Rule is not obſerved.

There is between the *Arms* and their *Bearers* a kind of Sympathy, inſomuch as he who diſhonourably or unreverently uſeth the Arms of any one, ſeemeth to have offered an affront to the Per-

Sympathy of Arms with their Bearers.

son of their Bearer, insomuch that according to the opinion of some *Authors*, their owner may right himself against such an Offender, *actione injuriarum*.

Antient Bearing.

As touching the antiquity of *Arms*, I shall give you a Brief account of some peculiar *Bearings*. The *Romans* chose the *Eagle* the greediest of all Birds: The *Phrigians* the *Sow*, a hurtful Beast: The *Thrasians Mars :* The antient *Goths* the *Bear :* The People of *Alani*, that invaded *Spain* the *Cat*, a greedy and crafty Beast : The Old *French* the *Lyon* : The *Saxons* the same ; but afterwards the *French* that inhabited *France* took the *Toad*, and the *Saxons* the *Horse* a warlike Beast, and now the *French* have the *Flower de-lis*, which they say was sent them by an Angel from Heaven to *Clovis*, the first Christian King of *France* : The *Flemins* did bear the *Bull*, in token of valiantness and hardiness. The Ensign of the King of *Antioch* was an *Eagle* holding a *Dragon* in his claws : That of *Pompey* a *Lion* with a Sword : That of *Attilla* was a Crowned *Gennet*, and the *Romans* themselves that were saved by Geese that watched in the Capitol, could not be moved for so great a Bene-

fit

fit received, to bear a *Goose* in their Enfigns.

There be of them alfo that fet in their Shields *Swords, Daggers, Halberts, Axes, Towers, Caftles, Engines,* and many other Inftruments of Homicide and Deftruction: Furthermore the *Enfigns* of the *Perfians* was a Bow and Quivers, likewife amongft the Heathen Gods, *Jupiter* chofe *Lightning*; *Neptune* the cripple toothed *Mace*; *Mars* the *Javeline*; *Bacchus* the *Spear* wrapped in *Boughs* and *Ivy*; *Saturn* the *Sieth*, and every one of thefe *Badges* of Arms, according to the nature of his *Cruelty, Raving, Violence, Mankood,* &c. As the Heralds do appoint, are fuppofed fome to be *Nobler Bearings* then others; for the more cruel and fierce the *Beaft* or *Fowl* is, the more Noble is that *Shield* efteemed, and thofe *Targets* or *Shields* that have milder things thereon, as *Trees, Flowers, Plants,* and the like, alfo the *Sun, Moon, Stars, Planets,* and other of the *Celeftial Spheres,* or fuch as be parted only with variety of colours, or charged with any of the *Honourable Ordinaries* only, as alfo by any *Artificial things,* made by the Invention of Man: Thefe and fuch like things are

A 4   not

not esteemed so Noble as the former, and are not so Antient *Bearings.*

Thus having briefly shewed the first Original Institution and Use of *Arms,* I shall proceed to the practick Exercise of these *Armorial Tokens ,* which appertain to the Office of a *Herald ,* and is termed *Armory,* and may be thus defined ; *Armory is an Art rightly prescribing the true knowledg and use of Arms.*

Definiti-on of Armory.

The skill of *Armory* consists in *Blazoning* and *Marshalling.*

Rules in Blazoning Coats.

By *Blazoning* is understood the displaying or expressing a *Coat* of *Arms* in its proper Colours and Metals , for to lay *Colour* upon *Colour, Metal* upon *Metal* is a great fault , and a different form of *Blazoning* makes the *Arms* not the same.

Rules in Martial-ling Coats.

By *Marshalling* is understood the joyning of divers *Arms* in one *Shield* , in which you must have a great care, but of this more when I treat of *Arms* joyned together.

You must use no repetition of words, but comprise them in as few as you can.

A *French Armorist* saith , that to *Blazon* , is to express what the Shapes , Kinds , and Colour of things born in

Arms

'*Arms* are, together, with their apt and proper *Significations*.

In the *Blazoning* of any *Coat* of *Arms*, always obferve this fpecial Rule, firft begin with the *Field*, and then proceed to the *Blazon* of the Charge, and if there be fundry things charged in the *Field*, whether they be of one or divers kinds, name that firft which is moft prædominate, and lyeth next the Field. and then that which is moft Remote.

The *Blazon* of *Arms* confifts in *Accidents* and *Parts*; and fuch *Accidents* are *Tincture* and *Differences*.

Tincture, as *Guillim* notes, is a variable hew of *Arms*, and is as well common to *differences* of *Arms*, as to *Arms* themfelves, and the fame is diftributed into *Colours* and *Furs*. Tincture.

Colours he faith is an external Dye, wherewith any thing is coloured or ftained; or elfe is the glofs of any body beautified with light; and the *Colour* here mentioned is both General and Special; by *General* is underftood the proper and natural colour of each particular thing, whether *Natural* or *Artificial*, of what kind foever they are Illuftrated, or fet forth in their external or proper Beauty. Colours.

Things

Things that are born in their natural *Colours* are to be blazoned proper, and not to mention the *Colours.*

Other things there are in *Armory* which have only names attributed unto them, and no *Colour* specified in the Blazoning thereof, the name being sufficient to express the same, although the form is all one and the same, which is in Resemblance like a round *Ball* or *Bullet*, the names of which are as followeth, with *Colours* appropriate to them.

1: *Besants*, whose Colour is Or.
2. *Plates*, Argent.
3. *Hurts*, Azure.
4. *Torteauxes*, Gules.
5. *Pellet* or *Agresses*, Sable.
6. *Pomeis*, Vert.
7. *Golpes*, Purpure.
8. *Orenges*, Tenne.
9. *Guzes*, Sanguine.

In these Nine are comprehended all the Colours usually made use of in *Bla-zonry.*

Terms for Colours. *Coats* of *Arms* are *Blazoned* by *Metals* and *Colours*; when they belong to *Gen-tlemen*, under the Degree of *Nobiles*

Mino-

Minores, as *Gentlemen*, *Esquires*, *Knights*
and *Baronets*; By *Precious-stones*, when
to those of the Nobility, as *Barons*, *Viscounts*, *Earls*, *Marquisses* and *Dukes*; and
by *Planets*, when to *Emperours*, *Kings*,
and *Soveraign Princes*.

Mettals and Colours.	*Precious Stones.*	*Planets.*
Or	Topaz	Sol
Argent	Pearl	Luna
Gules	Ruby	Mars
Azure	Saphir	Jupiter
Sable	Diamond	Saturn
Vert	Emerald	Venus
Purpure.	Amethist	Mercury
		(Head
Tenne	Jacynthe	Dragons
		(Tail.
Sanguine.	Sardonix.	Dragons

This

Or.

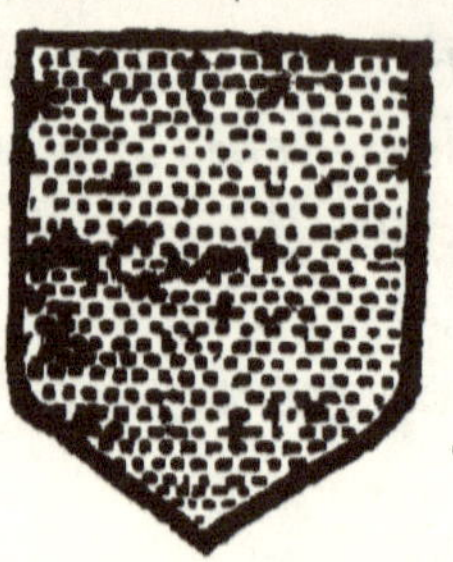

This in Arms is Blazo-
ned *Or*, and fignifies *Gold*
and the black Specks
in the Efcocheon do ex-
prefs the *Colour*. This
Metal is faid to Inchant
the Heart of Fools,
and Blind the Eyes of the Wife. Of
the excellency of this Metal, *Hefiodus*
thus writes, *Aurum eft in corporibus, ficut
Sol inter ftellas*; and as this *Metal* doth
exceed all others in Purity, Value and
Finenefs, fo ought the Bearer to endea-
vour to furpafs all others in Vertue
and Prowes.   The *Precious Stone* is *To-*

Topaz.   *paz*, which *Diafcorides* faith affwages
wrath and ill humors, and this Stone was
fet in the Breaft of *Aaron*.

Sol.   The *Planet* to which Gold is refem-
bled is *Sol*, of which the *Philofophers*
write, that as the Heart of Man is the
Nobleft, fo is this *Planet* more worthy
then any other, and as it were the com-
fort of them all.

The

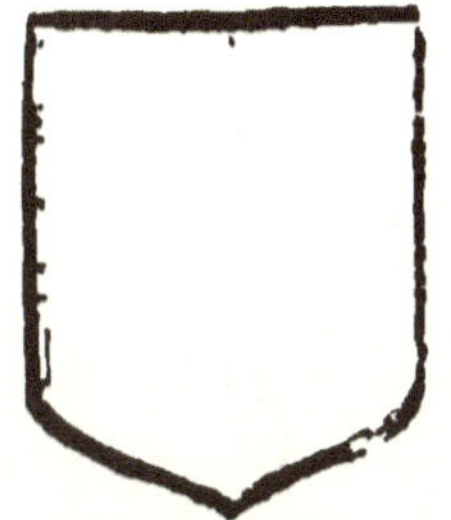

The Colour White is *Argent.*
reſembled to Light, and
is called Argent, this in
Dignity and Worth is
next to *Or,* and without
theſe two *Metals* no *Ar-*
mory can be good.   It ſignifies Hope, Innocency, Continence and
Temperance.   The Precious Stone is *Pearl.*
Pearl, which *Plato* ſaith hath a reſtora-
tive Vertue, and is food to man, which
is verifyed by *Joſephus,* who ſaith, that
when the City of *Jeruſalem* was beſieged
by *Titus Veſpaſianus,* the *Jews* lived ſome
time only upon *Pearls,* and *Ariſtotle* ſaith
it comforteth the Brain.

The *Planet* is *Luna,* which *Pliny* ſaith *Luna.*
is the Fairneſs of the Night, the Mother
of the Honour, and Lady of the Sea and
Times, She is alſo ſaid to be the changer
of the *Air* and *Winds,* and as the Scripture ſaith, She is the Ripener of, and In-
creaſer of Fruits, as appears by the be-
nediction of *Joſeph,* who was bleſt with
the ripe Fruits of the *Moon.*

The

Gules.

The word *Gules* signi-fieth Red, the Hatches downwards shews the Co-lour, which is of that Dignity, that it is used for a Vesture of Majesty and Dignity. and is used by the Judges and Chief Magistrates in their Seats of Judicature.

Ruby. The precious Stone is the *Ruby*, which neither Fire nor Water wasteth or spoyl-eth.

Mars. Its *Planet* is *Mars*, which of all others is the most Hot and Fiery, he is said to be the God of Battle.

Azure.

The word Azure sig-nifies Blew, and is ex-pressed by Hatches over-thwart the *Escocheon*; It is a Royal Colour repre-senting the Skie; it sig-nifies *Loyalty*, *Chastity*, and *Fidelity*. The *Precious Stone* is *Saphir*.

Saphir. which as *Isidore* saith, is both Noble and Excellent, being a remedy against Poy-son, and a Preserver of the Sight. The

Jupiter. *Planet* is *Jupiter*, which by his goodness, as *Martianus* saith, abateth the Malice

of

of *Saturn*, and augmenteth the goodnefs
of the others.

The word *Sable* figni-
fies *Black*, and is expref-
fed by crofs *Hatches* as in
the *Efcocheon*, and al-
though it doth reprefent
Mourning, yet is of a
good efteem in Armory.
This Colour fignifies Prudence, Conftancy and Heavinefs for the lofs of
Friends; the Precious Stone is the *Dia-*
mond, which of all other is of the great-
eft value, and is of that hardnefs, that
it cutteth all *Stones* and *Metals*. The
Planet is *Saturn*, the moft malevolent
of all others, and under whom are
brought forth Grave *Councellors*, great
Builders and good Houfe-keepers.

The word *Vert* is *Green*,
and is expreft by ftroaks
thwart ways, as in the
Efcocheon : This Colour
is moft delightful and
comfortable to the fight,
it fignifies *Love*, *Mirth*,
Peace, and *Concord*. The Precious Stone
is

Sable.

Diamond.

Vert.

Emerald.   is the *Emerald*, which hath in its self
Venus.   singular Vertues. The Planet is *Venus*
which is of temperature Cold and Moist,
and doth excite to Love.

Purpure.   *Purpure* is a Colour consisting of much **Red**, and a little **Black**, it hath its denomination from a Fish called in Latin *Purpura*. The Precious Stone

Amethist.   is the *Amethist*, which for its preciousness was set in the Breast of *Aaron*. The *Planet* is *Mercury*, which is of a goodly Temperature, being of quality good with good, and goeth with evil for Company sake.

Tenny.   *Tenny* or *Tauny* is a bright colour, and made of Red and Yellow, and is exprest by *Hatches* like the *Purpure*; Amongst the *French* this Colour is much in use, but not with us: The *Precious Stone*

Jacynthe.   is the *Jacynthe*, which is said to be of singular Vertue. This *Tenny* is com-

Dragons Head.   pared to the *Dragons Head*, which although it be not a *Planet*, yet in some respects hath the Nature of a *Planet*, and keeps its constant course in the *Zodiack* as they do.

San-

Sanguine is much like the colour of Sanguine. *Murrey*, and is made of *Lake*, with a little Spanish Brown, it is also exprest by Hatches as the *Purpure*, It is a Colour in use amongst the Knights of the *Bath*, as also amongst the *Sergeants* at Law in their Vestures. The *Precious Stone* to this Colour is the *Sardonix*, which St. *John* in the *Revelations* saith, shall be the sixth Stone in the Heavenly *Jerusalem*. The *Dragons Tayl* is appro- Dragons
Tayl. priate to this Colour, which though no *Planet*, yet in his Workings and Movings hath the effects of a *Planet* through all the Twelve Signs of the *Zodiack*.

Thus having treated of the *Metals*, and *Colours* used in *Heraldry*: I shall proceed next to *Furrs*, used as well in Doublings of the *Mantles* pertaining to *Coat Armour*, as in the Coat it self.

Furrs, according to *Guillim*, consists Furrs. of one Colour alone, or of more then one:

Furs that are Compounded of two Colours only, are sorted either.

    with *Black* and are either — Black mixt with *White* as *Ermine,* and *Ermines* Or Black mixt with *Yellow* as *Erminois* and *Pean,*

    Or without *Black* such are according to *Leigh*. — Vairy, *Argent* and *Azure*. and Verry, Or and Gules, or the like Colours.

But for the better explaining them ob-
serve these Examples following.

Ermine and Erme-
nois.

Ermine, that is the Field is Argent, and the Powdering is Sable.
    Ermenois, is when the Field is Or, and the Powdering is Sable.

Ermines and Pean.

Ermines, that is the Field is Sable, and the Powdering is Argent.
    Pean is when the Field is Sable, and the Powderings are Or.

Verry

Verry or *Vairy*, which is of two forts, that is if your *Vairy* do confift of Argent and Azure, then in Blazoning to fay *Vairy* is fufficient, but if it be compounded of any other Colours, they fay *Vairy* of fuch and fuch a Colour, naming them.

This Example is Blazoned *Potent-Counter·Potent*, or *Vairy Copy*, and the Colours muft be expreft as *Azure* and *Argent*, or the like.

In Antient times thefe *Doublings* or *Furs* were ufed for lineings of *Robes*, and *Mantles* of *Senators*, *Confuls*, *Kings* and *Emperors*.

Having in Brief given you the Examples of *Furrs*, I fhall next proceed to *Bordures*.

Examples of
BORDURES.

Bordures plain. THE First is Gules, a *Bordure* Or, although this *Bordure* is plain, yet in the Blazoning the word plain is to be omitted.

Engrailed 2. Sable, a *Bordure Engrailed* Argent, this is called Engrailed from the Latin word *Ingred or*, which signifies to go in, or to make entrance, or else from *Gradus*, which signifies a Step or Degree.

Invected. 3. Argent a *Bordure* Invected Azure This *Bordure* is quite contrary to the last, for as the other did enter into the Field, so contrariwise this doth, by the inversion of the points, into it self.

Indented. 4. Gules a *Bordure Indented* Argent. This is so called as being as it were composed of *Teeth*, and in the fashion of *Indentures*.

5. Azure

Bordures,—
Plaine and Charged.

5. Azure a *Bordure Counter-Componed* Argent and Gules. Note that *Counter-Compony* doth always confiſt of two *Tracts*, and no more, whereas that of *Checky* doth of three.

6. Vert a *Bordure Vairy*.

7. Or a *Bordure Checky* Argent and Sable.

8. Ermine a *Bordure Azure*, charged with eight *Plates*. Note that a *Plate* is always to be underſtood to be Argent, without expreſſing the Colour.

9. Gules a *Bordure* Sable, charged with three *Bendlets* Argent. What a *Bend* is ſhall be ſhewed when I come to ſpeak of *Bends*.

10. Ermine a *Bordure* Gobonated Or and Sable.

This is ſo termed as being in ſmall and equal Pieces.

11. Gules a *Bordure* Argent charged with *Verdoy of Trefoils* ſlipped proper, that is Vert.

12. Azure a *Bordure* quarterly com-poſed of *Purflew* Ermin, and *Counter-Compony*, Argent and Gules.

Theſe Examples may ſuffice, the more curious may be further ſatisfied in *Guillims* Diſplay of *Heraldry*, in the Chapter of *Bordures*. *Exam-*

Examples of

FILES and LABELS.

Files.   1. **A**RGENT a File with one *Label* Gules.

2. Azure a *File* of there *Lambeaux* Argent.

3. A File of five *Points* or *Lambeaux*, Azure.

4. Argent a File of three points in *Bend* Sable.

5. Three Files *Bar* ways Gules, the firſt having 5 Points, the Second 4, and the Laſt Tripple Pointed.

6. Argent a File iſſuing out of the *Chief*, without any Intermiſſion at all Sable.

Files, and Labells.

*Differences or Distinctions of Fa-
milies in Coat Armour.*

The First House.

The Elder Brother du-
ring the Life of his Father.　Label.

The Second Brother.　　　Crescent.

The Third Brother.　　Mullet.

The Fourth Brother.　　Martlet.

The Fifth Brother.　　Annulet.

The Sixth Brother.　　Flower-
delis.

B 4　　　　　　By

By thefe Differences every *Brother* or *Houfe* ought to obferve his due diffe-rence for the avoiding of contention in *Coat Armour.*

2*d.* Houfe.   The Frft Brother of the Second Houfe beareth a *Crefcent* charged with a *Label.* The Second Son of the Second Houfe, a *Crefcent* charged with another *Crefcent.* The Third Son of the Second Houfe a *Crefcent* charged with a *Mullet.* The Fourth Son of the Second Houfe a *Cre-fcent* charged with a *Martlet.* The Fifth Son of the Second Houfe a *Crefcent* charg-ed with an *Annulet.* And the Sixth Son of the Second Houfe, a *Crefcent* charged with a *Flower-delis.*

3*d,* Houfe.   The *Mullet*, which is the difference of the third Houfe is thus charged ; For the Firft Son with a *Label*; For the Se-cond with a *Crefcent* ; For the Third with a *Mullet* ; For the Fourth with a *Martlet*; For the Fifth with an *Annu-let* ; And for the Sixth with a *Flower-de lis.*

4*th.* 5*th.* and 6*th.* Houfer.   The *Martlet, Annulet* and *Flower de lis*, being the differences of the *Fourth, Fifth* and *Sixth* Houfes are charged for Diftinctions, as the *Mullet* is.

But

But Daughters are allowed to bear the *Arms* of their Fathers, without any of these *Differences* or *Distinctions.*

The PARTS of ARMS are the *Escocheon*, and the *Ornaments* without the Escocheon, as the *Mantle*, *Helmet* and *Crest.* *Parts of Arms.*

The *Accidents* in the *Escocheon* are *Points* and *Abatements.* *Accidents.*

Points are certain places in an *Escocheon*, diversly named, according to their several *Positions*, whereof some are in the *Middle*, and some *Remote.* Those in the Middle are in or near the Center of the *Escocheon*, and such are the *Honour*, the *Fess* and the *Nombril Points.* *Points.* *Middle Point.*

The *Fess Point* is in the exact Center of the *Escocheon*, *Fess Point.*

The *Honour Point* is next above the same in a direct Line, and the *Nombril Point* is next underneath the *Fess Point.* *Honour Point.*

Remote Points are those that are placed at a further distance from the Centre of the *Escocheon*, and of these some are Superior, and some Inferior. The Superior are those that have their being in the upper part of the *Escocheon*, and of these there are Middle and Extreams: The *Remote Point.*

3. The Middle is the precise middle of the *Chief*, between the two Extreams. The two Superior *Extream Points* do possess the Corners of the Chief part of the *Escocheon*, and are called the *Dexter* and *Sinister*.

Inferior Points.   The *Inferior Points* do possess the Base of the *Escocheon*, and of these there are also both Middle and Remote.

But for the better Explanation thereof, I have in an *Escocheon* placed *Letters* that answers to every one of the said *Parts* or *Points*.

Parts in the Escocheon.

A. Signifies the *Dexter. Chief-Point.*

B. The *Precise Middle Chief.*

C. The *Sinister Chief.*

D. The *Honour Point.*

E. The *Fess Point.*

F. The *Nombril Point.*

G. The *Dexter Base.*

H. The *Dexter Middle Base.*

I. The *Sinister Base Point.*

The knowledge of these *Points* are of great concernment, and ought to be well observed, for oft times they are occupied with sundry things of different kinds in one *Escocheon*.

Ex-

Abatements
of Honour.

Examples of

Abatements of HONOUR.

AN *Abatement* is an Accidental Mark annexed to *Coat Armour*, shewing some dishonourable quality or stain in the *Bearer*, whereby the Dignity of the *Coat Armour* is abased,

Abatements do consist in *Diminution* and *Reversing*. *Diminution* is a Blemishing of some particular Point of the *Escocheon*, by reason of some *Stain* and *Colour* which they must be always of, as *Sanguine* and *Tenne*, and never of *Mettal*, for then they are *Additions* of *Honour*. Now what these *Abatements* are, followeth.

    1. Argent a *Delph* Tenne: This Abatement is due to him that revoketh his challenge.

    2. Or, an *Escocheon* reversed Sanguin, Due for deflowring a Maid.

          3. The

[margin: Abatements. Delph. Escocheon reversed.]

Coat reversed.   3. The whole *Coat* Reversed *(viz.)* Sable a *Lyon Rampant*, Argent due to a *Traytor*.

Point Dexter.   4. Or, a *Point Dexter* Tenne, due for too much boasting of his *Martial Acts*.

Point in point.   5. Argent, a *Point in Point* Sanguine, due to a Coward.

Point Campion.   6. Or, a *Point Campion* Tenne, due to him that kills his Prisoner, after he hath yeilded himself and craveth Quarter.

Gore.   7. Argent, a *Gore Sinister* Tenne, due for flying from his *Colours*.

Gussets.   8. Or, two *Gussets* Sanguine, due to him that commits *Adultry*.

Plain point.   9. Argent, a *Plain Point* Tenne, due to him that tells Lyes to his *Prince*, or *General*.

Forms

Rewards, and Additions of Honour.

Forms of CHARGES:

On which *Rewards* and *Additions* of *Honour* are oft times placed in *COAT-ARMOUR*.

1. Gules, a *Canton* Or. — Canton.
   2. Argent, a quarter Azure. Quarter.
   3. Sanguine, a *Gyron* issuing from the Dexter-chief Argent. Gyron.
   4. Ermine, an *Escocheon* Gules. Escocheon.
   5. Argent two *Flasques* Azure. Flasques,
   6. Sable, a Star of eight *Rayse* or Points Or, between two *Flanches* Ermin, and is the Coat Armour of Sir *Henry Hobart* of *Blinkling* in *Norfolk,* Knight and Baronet. Flanches.
   7. Tenne two *Voyders* Or. Voyders.

CHAP.

CHAP. II.

Treats of the divers kinds of Esco-cheons, what the Field *and* Char-ges *are , the* Diversity *of* Char-ges, *and their* Common Accidents, *with their* Properties *and* Forms: *And lastly of the* Bearing *or* Using *the* Ordinaries *in* COAT AR-MOUR; *together with divers* Notes, Rules *and* Observations *to them belonging.*

Escoche-ons. Escocheons are either of one *Tin-cture* or more then one. Those that are of more then one, some are more predominate, and that is said to be predominate, when some on *Metal*, *Colour* or *Fur* is spread, or is understood to be spread all over the surface of the *Escocheon*, which is term-ed the *Field* or *Shield*; And in such *Esco-cheon cheons* as have in them more *Tinctures* then one (as most have) the *Field* and *Charge* must be observed. And in the *Blazoning*, first name the Field, and then the Charge thereon, and if there be several *Charges* (as oft times there is) then name the first which is nearest the Field.   *Tincture of the Field.*

. The Charge is that which possesseth the Field, whether it be *Sensitive* or *Vegetable*, *Natural* or *Artificial*, and is placed either throughout all the superficies of the *Escocheon*, or else in some special part of the same.   *The Charge.*

The common *Accidents* of *Charges* are *Adumbration* or *Transparency*; or they are *Transmutation* or *Counter-changing*.   *Common Accidents.*

The making of ORDINARIES consists of Lines diversly Composed. Lines are the matter whereof these *Ordinaries* are formed, and according to the divers *Tracts* and *Forms* of *Lines*, they receive their divers Shapes and variation of Names.   *Ordinaries.*

The property of these Lines are their *Rightness* or *Crookedness*.

A *Right Line* is carried equally throughout the *Escocheon* without rising, or falling, contrary to which is a crooked *Line*.

A

A *Crooked Line* is either Bunched or Cornered, according to these Examples.

Engrailed.

Invected.

Waved.

Crenelle or Embattuled.

Nebule.

Indented.

Dancette.

Of these and Streight Lines are composed the *Honourable Ordinaries* ; as also *Abatements* and *Rewards* of *Honour*.

The

The Honourable

ORDINARIES.

THE *Honourable Ordinaries* are the Cro*s*s, *Chief*, Fe*s*s, *Barr*, *Pale*, *Cheveron*, *Bend*, *Saltier* and *Es*cocheon, all which *s*hall be treated of in order.

The CROSS taketh up the fifth part of the *Escocheon*, but if charged then the third, and it is born as well Engrailed, Inve´ted, Wavey, or the like as plain, al*s*o 'tis born between a Charge, and charged, as the re*s*t of the *Ordinaries* are.

The CHIEF is *s*aid to be given to tho*s*e, that by their high merits have procured them chief places and e*s*teem among*s*t men. It mu*s*t contain the third part of the *Escocheon* in depth, and it is divided into a *Fillet*, which contains the fourth part of the *Chief*, and *s*tandeth in the *Chief Point*.

Honoura-
ble Ordi-
naries.

Cro*s*s.

Chief.

Fillet.

G

The

Fess. The **FESS** contains in breadth the third part of the *Escocheon*, and doth occupy the *Center* of the *Shield*. This hath formerly been taken for the Girdle of Honour, as dividing the Shield into two equal parts.

Bar. The **BAR** differeth from the *Fess* only in that it contains, but the fifth part of the *Shield*, whereas the *Fess* doth the

Closet. third. It is divided into the *Closet*, which contains the moity of the *Barr*,

Barulet. and the *Barulet* which is the half of the *Closet*.

  The **PALE** contains the third part of the *Eschocheon*. It is subdivided into a

Pale. *Pallet* which is the half of the Pale, and
Pallet. is never to be charged with any thing, either Quick or Dead, neither must it

Endorse. be parted; and into an *Endorse*, which is the fourth part of a *Pale*, and is not used but when the *Pale* is between two of them. If the *Pale* be upon any Beast, then you must say, *He is Debrused with the Pale*, but if the Beast be on the *Pale*, then say, *He is Supported of the Pale*.

Cheveron The **CHEVERON** Represents the *Rafters* of a House, and was in Antient time the Head attire of *Women Priests*. It takes up the fifth part of the Field,

and

and is fubdivided into the *Cheveronel*, Chevero-
nel.
which contains half a *Cheveron*, and
a *Couple Clofe*, which is the fourth part of Couple-
clofe.
a *Cheveron*, and is not born but by
Pairs, except there be a *Cheveron* between
them.

The **BEND** doth contain the fifth part Bend.
of the Field in Breadth if uncharged, but
if charged, then the third.

It is divided into a *Bendlet*, which is Bendlet.
limited to the fixth part of the *Shield*;
Into a *Garter*, which is the moity of a
Bend; Into a *Coft*, which is the fourth Coft.
part of a *Bend*; and into a *Ribon* the Ribon.
moity of a *Coft*.

There is alfo the *Bend Sinifter*, which Bend Sini-
fter.
goeth thwart the *Efcocheon* from the *Si-*
nifter Chief, to the *Dexter Bafe*, which
is quite contrary to the other *Bend*;
and this is fubdivided into the *Scrape*, Scrape.
which is half the *Bend*, and into the
Battune which is the fourth part of the Battune.
Bend; And this is the moft ufual Badg
of Illegitimacy; but note that the *Bat-*
tune doth not extend it felf quite thwart
the Shield, but wants fomething at both
fides, as by the example will appear.

The **SALTIER** Contains the fifth Saltier.
part of the Shield, but if charged then

the third.   The *Saltier* is said to be about the height of a Man, and was formerly used to Scale the Walls of a Town, and was driven full of Pins, which served for Steps.

This *Ordinary* as the rest is born *Engrailed, Wavey*, or the like, as also between Or, charged with a *Charge*.

An *Inescocheon* doth contain the fifth part of the Field, and must be placed in the *Fess point.* This is also termed an *Escocheon of Pretence*, and is so born by those that match with an *Heiress*, giving therein her *Coat* of *Arms*.

An Inescocheon.

Escocheon of Pretence.

Examples of the several

CROSSES

Most Usually born in *Coat* Armour.

Raynsford 1.   **A**Rgent a Cross sable born by Sir *Richard Raynsford* of *Dallington*

in

Crosses.

in *Northampton-shire*, Knight, late Lord Chief Juſtice of his Majeſties *Court* of Kings Bench.

Or, a *Croß* Vert, born by the Name of *Huſſey*.   Huſſey.

Ermine, a Croſs Sable, by the name of *Archer*.   Archer.

Argent, a Croſs Sable between four *Pellets*, born by Sir *Robert Clayton* of the City of *London*, Knight, Lord-Mayor thereof, *Anno* 1680.   Clayton.

2. Sable, a Croſs *Potence* Or, born by the Name of *Alleyn*.   Alleyn.

Azure, a Croſs *Potence* Or, by the Name of *Branchley*.   Branchley

Gules, a Croſs *Potence* Ermine, by the Name of *Norton*.   Norton.

Ermine, a Croſs *Potence* Azure, by the Name of *Lemynge*,   Lemynge.

Per Bend, Or and Sable, a Croſs *Potence* counterchanged by the Name of *Alman*.   Alman.

3. Azure, a Croſs *Potence* or *Potent Fitche* Or, born by *Etheldred*, King of the *Weſt Saxons*.

4. Sable, a Croſs *Patee* or *Forme* Argent, born by *Mapleſden*   Mapleſden

Gules, a Croſs *Patee* Argent, by the Name of *Croß*.   Croſs.

C 3   Ar-

Argent, a Cross *Patee Flowry* Sable,
Swinston. by the Name of *Swinston.*

Per Pale, Or and Gules, a Cross
Patee, Counterchanged by the Name of
Clopton. *Clopton.*

5. Or, a Cross *Patee* Gules, fimbri-
ated Sable, that is edged with another
Cross of a different Colour.

6. Or, on a Cheveron Gules, three
Crosses *Patee* or *Forme* of the Field, born
by *William Peck* of *Samford-Hall* in *Effex*, Esquire, Son and Heir of *Edward
Peck* of the said place, Sergeant at Law
deceafed.

Peck.

7. Ruby, a Cheveron between ten
Crosses *forme Pearl*, born by the Right
Honourable *George Berkeley*, Lord *Berke-
ley, Mowbray, Segrave* and *Bruce*, Ba-
Earl of ron of *Berkeley Caftle*, and Earl of *Berke-
Berkeley. ley*, &c.

Ruby a Cheveron Ermine between ten
Crosses forme, Pearl is born by the Right
Honourable *Mawrice Berkeley*, Baron
Berkeley of *Rathdown*, and Viscount *Fitz
Viscount Harden* of *Bear haven* in *Ireland.*
Fitz Hard-
ing. Also by the Right Honourable *John*
Lord Lord *Berkeley*, Baron of *Straton* in *Somer-
Berkeley. fet-fhire*, &c.

8. Azure

8. Azure, a *Cross Moline* Or, born by Sir *John Molineux* of *Tavershal* in *Nottinghamshire*, Baronet.

Molineux.

Azure, a Cross *Moline* Argent, by the Name of *Trelesk*.

Trelesk.

Gules, a Cross *Moline* Or, by the Name of *Berneston*.

Berneston

Argent, a Cross *Moline* Gule, by the Name of *Vudal*.

Vudal.

9. Sable, a Cross *Couped* or *Pierced* Or, by the Name of *Grill*.

Grill.

Note that *Piercings* are born round, as in this example, as also four square, and *Lozenge ways*.

10. Ermine, a Cross *Patonce* Sable, born by *Jonathan Goddard* Doctor in Physick, and Fellow of the Colledge of Physitians.

Goddard.

Gules, a Cross *Patonce* Argent, by the Name of *Latimer*.

Latimer.

Argent a Cross *Patonce* Sable, by the Name of *Banester*.

Banester.

Vert a Cross *Patonce* Or, by the Name of *Boydel*.

Boydel.

Sable, a Cross *Patonce* Or, by the Name of *Mannock*.

Mannock.

Azure, a Cross *Patonce* Or, by the Name of *Ward*.

Wa.d.

Quar-

Quarterly Gules and Azure, a Cross
Wenman. *Patonce* Or, born by Sir *Richard Wenman*
of *Caswel* in *Oxford-shire*, Baronet.

11. Argent, a Cross *Bottony* Sable,
Winwood born by *Richard Winwood* of *Ditton* Park
in *Buckingham-shire* Esq; Son and Heir
of the Right Honourable Sir *Ralph Winwood* Knight, Principal Secretary of State
to King *James*, and Embassador *Ledger*
to the States of the *United Provinces*.

12. Argent, a Cross *Flowry* Sable,
Copley. and is the Coat of Sir *Godfrey Copley* of
Sproadbrough in *York-shire* Baronet.

13. Sable, a Cross *Raguled* Or, by the
Stoway. Name of *Stoway*.

Argent, a Cross *Raguled* Sable, by the
Wroth. Name of *Wroth*.

14. Argent, a Cross *Wavey voided* Sa-
Ducken-
field. ble, by the Name of *Duckenfield*.

15. Azure, a Cross *Moline* Or, void-
ed throughout; this with the addition
of Cross *Croslets* Or, dispersed in the
Knowles. Field, is the Coat of *Knowles*, of which
Family is the Right Honourable *Charles*
Earl of Earl of *Banbury*, Viscount *Wallingford*,
Banbury. and Baron *Knowles* of *Greys*.

16. Or

16. Or, a Crofs *Croflet* Gules, by the Name of *Taddington*.

Argent, a Crofs *Croflet* Sable by the Name of *Wickerley*.

Argent, a Crofs *Croflet* Gules, by the Name of *Brightley*.

Vert, a Crofs *Croflet* Or, by the Name of *Bury*.

Sable, a Crofs *Croflet* Ermine, by the Name of *Durant*.

17. Argent, a *Cheveron* between three Crofs *Croflets* Gules, born by *Richard Stern* of *White Cliff* in *York-fhire* Efquire, Son to his Grace, *Richard* late Lord *Arch-Bifhop* of *York* Deceafed.

18. Azure, a *Fefs Dauncette* Ermine, between fix Crofs *Croflets* Argent, born by Sir *Thomas Barnardifton* of *Kediton* in *Suffolk*, Knight and Baronet, By Sir *Samuel Barnardifton* of *Brightwel* Hall in the faid County Baronet.

19. Argent, a Cheveron Azure between three Crofs *Croflets* Fitche Gules, born by Sir *John Buckworth* of *London*, Knight.

20. Argent, a Crofs *Couped* Sable, charged with another Or.

21. Azure

21. Azure, a Cross *Engrailed* Ermine,
Stoughton born by *Nathaniel Stoughton* of St. *Johns*
near *Warwick*, Esquire.

22. Sable a Cross *Engrailed* Or, in the
dexter quarter a *Mullet* Argent by the
Name of *Peyton*, of which Family is Sir
Peyton. *Thomas Peyton* of *Knolton in Kent*, Baronet.

By Sir————*Peyton* of *Doddington* in
Cambridg-shire, Baronet: and Sir *Robert
Peyton* of *East Barnet* in *Hartford-shire*,
Knight.

23. Sable, a Cross *Engrailed* Argent,
in the Dexter Quarter an *Escallop shell*
Pagit. of the second, born by *Justinian Pagit* of
Grays-Inn, Esquire.

24. Azure, a *Taw* Argent Ermine, or
a cheif indented Gules, 3 Taws Or,
born by *Edward Thurland* Esquire, only
Thurland. Son of Sir *Edward Thurland* of *Reygate*
in *Surrey*, Knight, one of the Barons
of his Majesties Court of *Exchequer*,
Deceased.

25. Azure, a Cross *Flury* Argent, by
Cheney. the Name of *Cheney*.

Sable, a Cross *Flury* Or, by the Name
Manox. of *Manox*.

26. Gules, a Cross *Pall* Argent.

27. Azure,

Cheifs, with Charges
thereon.

27. Azure, a Cross *Avelane* Argent.

28. Gules, a Cross *Furche* Or.

29. Or, a Cross *Ankred* Sable.

Thus much for *Crosses* which may be born between, or Charged with a *Charge,*

Examples of

CHIEFS.

1. OR, a *Chief* Gules, born by Sir *Martin Lumley* of *Bradfield* in *Essex* Baronet.

Lumley.

2. Azure, a *Chief* Engrailed Or.

3. Argent, a Chief Invected Vert.

4. Saphir, a *Chief Indented* Topaz; born by his Grace *James* Duke, Marquess and Earl of *Ormond*, Earl of *Ossery* and *Brecknock*, Viscount *Thurles*, Baron of *Arklow* and *Lanthony*, Lord High Steward of his Majesties *Houshold, Knight* of the Honourable Order of the *Garter*,

Duke of Ormond.

Chan-

Chancellor of the Univerſity of *Oxford*, Lord Leiutenant of *Ireland*, and one of the Lords of his Majeſties moſt Honourable *Privy Conncel*, &c.

Earl of Oſſery.

By The Right Honourable *James* Lord *Butler* Baron of *More Park* in *England*, and Earl of *Oſſery* in *Ireland*, Grand Child to his Grace *James* Duke of *Ormond*.

Earl of Arran.

By the Right Honourable *Richard* Earl of *Arran*, Viſcount *Tulough*, Baron of *Clougrenan* in *Ireland*, and Baron *Butler* of *Weſton* in *England*, ſecond Son to his Grace *James* Duke of *Ormond*, and Lord Leiutenant of *Ireland*, *Anno*, 1683.

5. Azure, a *Chief Nebule* Argent.

6. Gules a *Chief Crenelle* or *Embattuled* Or.

7. Ermine, a *Chief Dauncette* Sable.

8. Vert, a *Chief Wavey* Or.

9. Ermine, a *Chief* Quarterly Or and

Peckham. Gules, by the Name of *Peckham*.

10. Or, a *Chief Checky* Argent and Azure.

11. Gules, a *Chief* Argent *ſurmounted* of another Or.

12. Argent, a *Chief* Sable, in the nether part thereof a *Fillet* Argent.

13. Sa-

13. Sable, a *Chief* Or , charged with a *Shapournet* Ermine.

14. Azure , three *Barrs* Argent , in Chief three *Bezants* , born by Sir *Rich. Atkins* of *Much Hadham* in *Hartfor-shire*, Atkins. Knight and Baronet.

15. Azure , on a *Chief* Or , three *Martlets* Gules, born by Sir *William Wray* Wray. of *Ashby* in *Lincoln-shire*, Baronet.

By Sir —— *Wray* of *Glentworth* in the said County Baronet.

This *Ordinary* is subject to a *Charge*,
as the others are.

Examples

Examples of

FESSES and BARRS.

Eliot.   1. Azure a *Fess* Or, by the Name of *Eliot*.

Barnaby.   Ermine a *Fess* Gules, by the Name of *Barnaby*.

Colvil.   Or, a *Fess* Gules, by the Name of *Colvil*.

Pennington.   2. Ermine, a *Fess Dauncette* Sable, by the Name of *Pennington*.

West.   Argent, a *Fess Dauncette* Sable, by the Name of *West*.

Bengham.   Azure, a *Fess Dauncette* Argent, by the Name of *Bengham*.

Somner.   Vert a *Fess Dauncette* Ermine, by the Name of *Somner* of *Kent*.

Nevil.   Argent, a *Fess Dauncette* Gules, by the Name of *Nevil* of *Leicester*.

3. Gules, a *Fess Wavey* Argent.

4. Argent, a *Fess Humid* Sable.

5. Argent,

Fefses, Barrs
&c.

5. Argent, a *Fess per Fess Indented* Vert and Sable, between two *Cottizes* counterchanged, by the Name of *Huddy* of *Dorsetshire*.

6. *Per Fess Indented* Or and Azure, by the Name of *Saunders*.

7. Parted *per Fess* Sable and Argent, a *Fess Batile Counter-Battled*, Counterchanged.

8. *Per Fess* Or and Argent, a *Fess Netule* Gules, by the Name of *Antefbed*.

9. Argent, on a *Fess* between a double Cottize Gules, three Griffons Heads erazed Or, born by Sir *Robert Dashwood* of *Norbrook* and *Wickham* in *Oxfordshire*, Knight.

And by *Samuel Dashwood* of the City of *London* Esquire, now Sheriff of the said City.

10. Ruby, 4 *Fussils* in *Fess* Pearl, born by the Right Honourable *George* Lord *Carteret*, Baron of *Hawnes* in *Bedfordshire* &c.

And by Sir *Philip Carteret* of St. *Ouen* in the Isle of *Jarsey* Baronet.

11. Gules, a *Fess Wavey* between 3 Flower delis Or, born by Sir *William Hicks* of *Ruckolls* in *Essex*, Knight and Baronet.

12. Or

12. Or, on a *Fess* Azure, three *Garbs* of the Field, born by *James Vernon* of St. *Martins in the Field* in *Middlesex*, Esquire, descended from the *Vernons* of *Cheshire*.

Burkin.

13. Argent, a *Barr* Azure, born by Captain *James Burkin* of *London*, Esquire.

14. Topaz, three *Barrs Wavey* Ruby, born by the Right Honourable *James* Earl of *Perth*, Lord *Drummond* and *Stobhall*, Steward of *Strathern* and *Balahidder* by Inheritänce; Lord Justice General of the Kingdom of *Scotland*, one of the extraordinary Lords of the Session, and one of the Lords of his Majesties most Honourable Privy Councel for the said Kingdom.

Basset.

Barry Wavey of six Or and Gules, born by *John Basset* of *Heanton Punchardon* in *Devonshire*, Esquire.

15. Ermine, a *Croslet* Sanguine.

16. Sable, a *Barulet* Argent.

Example

Pales, Pallets &c.

Examples of
PALES.

1. Gules, a *Pale* Or, by the Name of *Grandmain*.   Grandmain.

2. Azure, a *Pallet* Argent.

3. Vert, an *Endorſe* Or.

4. Argent, a *Pale Lozenge* Sable, by the Name of *Savage*.   Savage.

Gules, a *Pale Lozenge* Argent, by the Name of *Manduit*.   Manduit.

5. Argent, a *Pale indented* Vert, by the Name of *Dixon*.   Dixon.

6. Argent, a *Pale Flory* Counterchanged Sable.

7. Gules, a *Pale Radiant* Or, by the Name of *Coleman*.   Coleman.

8. *Party per Pale* Argent and Sable, a Pale Counterchanged.

9. Argent, three *Pallets Wavey* Sable, by the Name of *Downes*.   Downes.

D

10. Ar-

10. Argent, a *Pale* between two *In-dorses* Gules.

11. Paly of six Topaz and Saphir, a *Canton* Ermine, born by the Right Hononrable *Robert* Lord *Shirley*, Baron *Fer-rers*, of *Chartley*, &c.

Lord *Fer-rers*.

12. Argent, on a *Pale* Sable, a Congers Head Erected and Couped Or, born by Sir *Bernard Gascoyn*, Knight.

Gascoyn.

Note that such *Ordinaries* as are either of themselves, or else by reason of some charge imposed on them, do challenge the third part of the *Field*, are exempted from this kind of Bearing one besides another, of such the Field can conteyn but one of them at once, but their *Derivatives* and *Subdivi-sions* may well be sorted in the same *Es-cocheon*, as a *Pale* between two *Endor-ses*, a *Bend* between two *Cottizes*, and such like.

Cheverons,

Examples of
CHEVERONS.

1. **G**Ules a *Cheveron* Argent, born by *Thomas Fulford* of *Fulford* in *Devonshire* Esquire.   *Fulford.*

Argent, a *Cheveron* Azure by the name of *Swillington.*   Swilling-ton.

Or a Cheveron Sable by the name of *Heningfield.*   Hening-field.

Argent, a *Cheveron* Gules by the name of *Trye.*   Trye.

2. Ermine, a *Cheveron couped* Sable, by the name of *Jones.*   Jones.

3. Or a *Cheveron* in chief Azure.

4. Sable, a *Cheveron Rompe* Argent.

5. Azure a *Cheveron engrailed voyded* Or, by name of *Dudley.*   Dudley.

6. Argent, two *Cheverons* Sable, born by Sir *Joseph Ash* of *Twittenham* in *Mid-dlesex* and of *Downton* in *Wiltshire* Baro-net.   Ash.

By *Samuel Ash* of *Langley-Burwel* in *Wiltshire*, Esq.

By *William Ash* of *Hatchbury* in the said County Esq.

And by *John Ash* of *Fifield* in the said County, Esq.

Bagot. Ermine, two *Cheverons* Azure, born by Sir *Walter Bagot* of *Blithfield* in *Staffordshire*, Baronet.

Mounson. Or, two *Cheverons* Gules, born by Sir *John Mounson* of *Burton* in *Lincolnshire*, Knight of the Bath and Baronet.

Fanner. Ermine, two *Cheverons* Gules, by the Name of *Fanner*.

Lewkener 7. Azure, three *Cheverons* Argent, born by *John Lewkenor* of *West Dean* in *Sussex* Esq.

Lougher. Argent, three *Cheverons* Gules, born by *Richard Lougher* of *Tytleston* in *Clamorganshire*, Esq.

Horne. Gules, three *Cheverons* Or, by the Name of *Horn*.

8. Argent, three *Cheverons* reversed Gules.

9. Argent, a *Cheveron Enarched* Gules.

10. Azure, three *Cheverons* braced in the base of the *Escocheon*, Or, by the *Fitz-hugh.* Name of *Fitz-Hugh*.

11. Ermine,

Bends .

11. Ermine, on a *Cheveron* Gules, three Cinquefoils Or, born by *Skepper* of *Skepper,* *Lincolnshire.*

12. Gules, a *Cheveron* engrailed between three Owles Argent, born b; Sir *George Hewytt* of *Pishobury* in *Hartford-shire,* Baronet.

13. *Ter Cheveron* Azure and Argent, in Chief two *Falcons* Volant Or, by the Name of *Stephens,* and is born by *Thomas Stephens,* Esquire, Son and Heir of Sir *Thomas Stephens* of little *Sodbury* in *Glocestershire,* Knight.

14. Vert, a *Cheveronel* Argent.

15. Ermine, a *Coupee-Close,* Gules.

Examples of
BENDS.

1. **O**R, a *Bend* Azure, by the Name of *Caltherupe.*

Colembert.   Gules, a *Bend* Or, by the Name of *Colembert*.

Kendal.   Argent, a *Bend* Vert, by the Name of *Kendal*.

Cottel.   Or, a *Bend* Gules, by the Name of *Cottel*.

Ratcliff.   2. Argent, a *Bend* Engrailed Sable, born by Sir *Francis Ratcliff* of *Dilston* in *Northumberland*, Baronet.

Culpeper.   Argent, a *Bend* Engrailed Gules, by the Name of *Culpeper*, and is the Coat of the Right Honourable *Thomas* Lord *Culpeper* Baron of *Thonway*.

It is also born by Sir *Thomas Culpeper* of *Preston Hall* in the Parish of *Aylesford* in *Kent* Baronet.

Grove.   Argent, a *Bend* Engrailed Azure, by the Name of *Grove*.

Clark.   Or, a *Bend* Engrailed Azure, by the Name of *Clark*.

Marshal.   Gules a *Bend* Engrailed Or, by the Name of *Marshal*.

Gules, on a *Bend* Argent, three *Crosses Patte* or *Forme* Sable, is born by Sir *John Rerersby* of *Thrikergh* in the West Riding of *Yorkshire*, Baronet, Governour of the City of *York*.

Cutts.   Argent, on a *Bend* Engrailed Sable, three *Plates* born by *John Cutts* of *Arks-*

den

don in *Eſſex*, and of *Childerly* in *Cambridgeſhire*, Eſq.

Argent a *Bend Wavey* Sable, born by *Henry Wallop* of *Farleigh-wallop* in *Hampſhire*, Eſq. — Wallop.

3. Gules, a *Bend Wavey* between two *Cottizes* Or *Coſts*, Argent by the Name of *Etton*. — Etton.

Azure, a *Bend Wavey* Cottized Argent, by the Name of *Keynes*. — Keynes.

Sable, a *Bend* Engrailed Cottized Argent, by the Name of *Willington*. — Willington.

Azure, a *Bend* Engrailed Argent, Cottized Or, by the Name of *Forteſcue*. — Forteſcue.

4. Sable, a *Bend* Flory Argent, by the Name of *High-Lord*. — Highlord.

Sable, a *Bend* Flory Or, by the Name of *Bromfleet*. — Broomfleet.

5. *Per Bend* Sable and Argent, a *Bend Ragule* Counter changed by the Name of *Strangman*. — Strangman,

6. Vert, a *Bend Lozenge* Or, by the Name of *Knight*, of *Hampſhire*. — Knight.

Sable, a *Bend Lozenge* Argent, by the Name of *Lenthal* of *Oxfordſhire*. — Lenthal.

Ermine, a *Bend Lozenge* Gules, by the Name of *Plumley* of *Devonſhire*. — Plumley.

7. Sable, a *Bend* engrailed between six *Cinquefoyls* Or, born by *Tho.* Povey Esquire, one of the *Masters of Requests* to his Majesty King *Charles* the Second.

Povey.

8. Ermine, a *Bend* voided Gules, by the Name of *Ireton.*

Ireton.

9. Or, two *Bendlets* Azure, by the Name of *D'oyly,* and is born by Sir *John D'oyley* of *Chisleyhampton* in *Oxfordshire,* Knight, by *Christopher* D'oyley of *Alderbury* in the said County Esquire, and by *Laud D'oyley* of St. *Giles* in the Fields, in *Middlesex,* Gent.

D'oyley.

Or, two *Bendlets* Gules, born by the Name of *Tracy.*

Tracy.

Or, two *Bendlets* Engrailed Sable, by the Name of *Brantwait.*

Braintwaite,

10. Azure, three *Bendlets* Wavey Azure, born by Sir *Thomas Wilbraham* of *Woodhey* in *Cheshire,* Baronet.

Wilbraham.

11. *Bendy* of six Pieces Argent and Gules.

12. Or, a *Garter* Gules.

13. Argent, a *Cost* or *Cottize* Sable.

14. Or, a *Ribon* Gules.

15. Argent a *Bend Sinister* Sable.

16. Azure, a *Scrape* Argent.

17. Gules, a *Battune* Argent.

Exa...

Saltiers,

Examples of
SALTIERS.

1. **P**Earl, a *Saltier* Ruby, born by the Right Honourable *Charles* Lord *Gerard*, Baron of *Brandon* and Earl of *Maxfield*, &c.

By the Right Honourable *John Fitz-Gerard*, Earl of *Kildare*, Primier Earl of the Kingdom of *Ireland*.

By the Right Honourable *Digby*, Lord *Gerard* Baron of *Gerards Bromley*, and Lord of *Dutton*.

By Sir *Francis Gerard* of *Harrow-hill* in *Middlesex*, Knight and Baronet.

By *Gilbert Gerard* Coffein of *Brafferton Hall* in the *North Riding* of *Yorkshire*, Esquire, Son and Heir to Sir *Gilbert Gerard*, Knight and Baronet.

Ruby, a *Saltier Pearl*, born by the Right Honourable *George* Lord *Nevil*, Ba-

Earl of Maxfield.

Earl of Kildare.

Lord Gerard.

Bergavenny.

Baron of *Bergavenny* in *Monmouth-shire,* but the Family of the *Nevils* beareth in the middle of the Saltier a Rose Gules for a Distinction.

Dering.

Or a *Saltier* Sable, born by the Right Honourable Sir *Edward Dering* of *Surrenden Dering* in *Kent*, Baronet, one of the Lords Commissioners of his Majesties Treasury, *&c.*

Baldwin.

Argent, a *Saltier* Sable, born by *Martin Baldwin* of *Castle Geshel* in Kings County in *Ireland*, Esquire.

York.

Azure, a *Saltier* Argent, born by Sir *William York* of *Burton Pedwarding* in *Lincolnshire*, Knight.

Nevil.

Gules, a *Saltier* Argent, charged with a Rose of the Field, born by the Name of *Nevill*.

Ducket.

Sable, a *Saltier* Argent, born by *Thomas Ducket* of *Stephmorden* in *Cambridgshire*, Esquire.

Hunt.

Vert, a *Saltier* Or, born by the Name of *Hunt*.

Gage.

Per Pale Azure and Gules, a *Saltier* Argent, by the Name of *Gage*.

Earl of Scarsdale.

2. Pearl; on a *Saltier* Engrailed Diamond, 9 *Annulets* Topaz, born by the Right Honourable *Robert Leak* Earl of *Scarsdale*, and *Baron Deyncourt*.

Vert,

Vert, a *Saltier* Engrailed Argent , by the Name of *Hawley*.

Hawley.

And is born by the Right Honourable *Francis* Lord *Hawley*, and by *Henry Hawley* of *Branford* in *Middlesex*, Esquire.

Argent, a *Saltier* Engrailed Sable, born by Sir *George Middleton* of *Leighton* in *Lancashire*, Baronet.

Middleton

3. Parted *per Saltier* Argent and Gules, a *Saltier* Counterchanged.

4. Azure, a *Saltier* quarterly quartered Or and Argent, being the Arms of the Episcopal See of *Bath* and *Wells*.

Bath and Wells.

5. *Per Pale* Argent and Azure, a *Saltier* Counterchanged by the Name of *Hodbonel*.

Hodbonel.

6. Gules on a *Saltier* Or, another Vert, by the Name of *Andrews*.

Andrews.

7. Gules, a *Saltier Cleche*, that is piered through, Or.

8. *Per Pale*, Argent and Gules, three *Saltiers* Counterchanged, born by *Lane* of *London*.

Lane.

9. *Girony* of four Argent and Gules, a *Saltier* between as many *Cross Croslets* all Counterchanged, born by *Roger Twisden* of *Bradborn* in *Kent*, Esquire, Eldest Son to Sir *Thomas Twisden*, Knight and Baronet, one of his Majesties Justices of Kings Bench.

Twisden.

Ex-

Examples of

INESCOCHEONS
and
ORLES.

1. ERmine an *Inescocheon* Gules.

2. Or, an *Orle* Azure, by the Name of *Bertram*.

Bertram.

3. Argent, an *Orle* Engrailed on the Innerside Gules.

4. Gules, an *Orle* Engrailed on both sides Or.

5. Argent, an *Orle* of three Peices Sable.

6. Argent, three *Escocheons* Sable, by the Name of *Lowdham*.

Lowdham

7. Topaz a Lyon Rampant, and Treasure of *Scotland* Ruby, within a Border gobonated Pearl and Saphir, this is the Coat of the Right Honourable

Alexander

Inescocheons,
and Orles.

Alexander Earl of *Morray*, Lord *Doun* Earl of
and *Abernethe* in *Scotland*, and one of his *Morray.*
Majesties principal Secretaries of State
for that Kingdom.

8. *Topaz*, a Lion Rampant cut in pieces at the Joynts Ruby, within a Treasure of *Scotland* Saphir, born by the Right Lord
Honourable *Richard* Lord *Maitland*, Lord *Maitland.*
Justice *Clarke* of the Kingdom of *Scot-*
land, one of the Lords of his Majesties
most Honourable Privy Councel for that
Kingdom, and Eldest Son to the Right
Honourable *Charles* Earl of *Lauderdale*,
&c.

9. Gules, an *Inescocheon* Argent, within
an *Orle* of *Cinquefoyls* Or, born by Do- Chamber-
ctor *Hugh Chamberlain* Doctor in Physick lain.
in Ordinary, to his Majesty King *Charles*
the Second, and by his Brother Doctor
John Chamberlain, Doctor in Physick.

Examples of
PILES.

THE *Pile* is an Ordinary consisting of a twofold Line, formed like a *Wedg*, and is an Antient Addition to *Armory*, being that which makes all *Foundations* and *Fortifications* sure and Firm, especially upon Moorish and Watry Grounds.

The Examples follow.

1. Or a *Pile* Engrailed Sable, born by the Name of *Waterhouse*.

Waterhouse.

2. Azure, a *Pile* Ermine, born by Sir *Cyrill Wyche* of *Flansford* in *Surry*, Knight, sometime *Embassadour* at *Constantinople*, for his Majesty King *Charles* the First.

Wyche.

Azure, a *Pile* Or, by the Name of *Aldham*.

Aldham.

Or, A *Pile* Azure, by the Name of *Bagginton*.

Baggington.

Sable

Piles.

Sable, a *Pile* Ermine, by the Name Moriswith.
of *Morifwith*.

3. Ermine, two *Piles* in point Diamond, born by the Right Honourable *John* Lord *Haughton*, Eldeſt Son to the Right Honourable *Gilbert* Earl of *Clare*, &c. Lord Haughton,

And is alſo born by the Right Honourable *Francis* Lord *Holles*, Baron *Holles* of *Ifield* in *Suſſex*. Lord Holles.

3. Argent three *Piles*, meeting near the baſe of the *Efcocheon* Azure, by the Name of *Bryan*, Bryan.

Or, three *Piles* Gules, by the Name of *Baſſet*. Baſſet.

Azure, three *Piles* Or, by the Name of *Salbourn*. Salbourn.

Azure, three *Piles* Gules by the Name of *Gildeſborough*. Gildeſborough.

Argent, three *Piles* waved Gules, by the Name of *Candiſh*. Candiſh.

Ermine, three *Piles waved* Gules, by the Name of *Gernon*. Gernon,

Ermyne, three *Piles* Engrailed Sable, by the Name of *Cade*. Cade.

5. Argent, three *Piles*, one iſſuing out of the *Chiefe*, between two others, tranſpoſed, or reverſed Sable, born by Captain *Richard Hulfe* of *Betherſden* in *Kent*, Eſquire. Hulfe.

6. Ar-

6. Argent, a *Pile* waved, issuing out of the Dexter Corner of the *Escocheon* Bendways Or, by the Name of *Aldham*.

7. Argent, a *Pile* in Bend, issuing out of the Dexter Corner of the *Escocheon* Sable, *Cottized Engrailed* Gules.

8. Argent, a *Triple Pile* flowry on the tops Sable, issuing out of the Sinister Base in *Bend*, towards the Dexter Corner.

9 Or, on a *Pile* Vert, three *Wheat-Sheaves* of the Field, born by Sir *Anthony Oldfield* of *Spalding* in *Lincolnshire*, Baronet.

Aldham. (margin)

Oldfield. (margin)

Partitions of

EXAMPLES.

PArtitions are such in which there is no *Tincture*, that is *Metal*, *Colour*, or *Fur* predominating in them, and are formed of sundry sorts of *Lines* of *Partition*,

Partitions.

tition, occafioning oft times *Counter-changing* and *Tranfmutation*, and thefe kinds of *Bearing* are fubject to be born *Wavey, Engrailed*, or the like : for Example.

1. Parted *per Pale* Argent and Gules, by the Name of *Walgrave*.   Walgrave

2. *Per Fefs* Or and Azure.

3. *Per Bend Embattuled* Pearl and Ruby, born by the Right Honourable
Boyle Lord *Clifford*, Eldeft Son to the Lord *Clifford.* Right Honourable *Richard Boyle* Earl of *Burlington*, and Baron *Clifford* of *Lanf-borough* in *England,* Earl of *Corke,* Vifcount *Dungarvan,* and Baron *Youghal* of *Ireland,* &c.

And by the Honourable *Robert Boyle* Boyle. of *Staulbridge* in *Dorfet-fhire* Efquire, Brother to the Right Honourable the Earl of *Burlington.*

Per Bend Or and Vert, by the Name of *Hawley*.   Hawley.

4. Quarterly Ermine and Sable, born by *John Stanhope* of *Elvefton* in *Derby-* Stanhope. *fhire,* Efquire.

Some Blazon this Coat parted *per Crofs.*

5. *Per Bend Sinifter* Argent and Azure.

E   6. *Per*

6. *Per Cheveron* Sable and Argent, born by Sir *Willoughby Aston* of *Aston* in *Cheshire*, Baronet.

Aston.

7. *Per Pile* in Point Or and Sable. The *Pile* part of this *Coat* may be charged, but no other part thereof, and that may be used as one only Coat.

8. *Per Pale* Travers, Argent and Gules.

9. Parted *Per Pile* Transposed Or, Gules and Sable. This is a Bearing rarely met with.

10. *Per Saltier* Gules and Ermine, by the Name of *Restwold*.

Restwold:

11. *Per Pale* and *Base* Gules, Argent and Sable, a Bearing unusual.

12. *Girony* of 6 pieces Or and Azure.

13. *Girony* of eight pieces Topaz and Diamond, and is born by the Right Honourable *Alchibald* Lord *Lorn*, Eldest Son to the Right Honourable *Archibald* Earl of *Argile*, Lord *Kintire Champbel* and *Lorn*, &c.

Lord *Lorn.*

14. *Per Pale* and *Cheveron* Argent and Gules.

15. *Chappe* Or and Vert Counterchanged.

From *Partitions* I shall proceed to *Counterchanges,* which doth also admit of a
Charge

Counterchanges.

Charge, as thefe Examples will Demon-
ftrate.

Examples of

COUNTERCHANGES.

1. **O**R a *Crofs* parted *per Pale* Gules
and Sable, by the Name of
Brook.   **Brook.**

2. *Per Pale,* Argent and Sable, a Pale
Counterchanged.

3. *Per Pale* Argent and Azure, *per
Bend Counterchanged;* this the French
Armorift term *Tranche.*

4. *Per Pale* Argent and Gules, a *Bend
Counterchanged* by the Name of *Chau-
cer.*   **Chaucer.**

5. *Paly* of fix Argent and Sable, a
Chief Counterchanged.

6. *Per Fefs* Gules and Argent, a *Pale
Counterchanged* by the Name of *Lavi-* **Lavider.**
der.

                    7. *Parted*

7. *Parted per Pale* Or and Gules, three *Roundels* Counterchanged.

8. *Per Fess* Argent and Vert, a *Pale* Counterchanged three *Lyons Heads* Erazed Gules, born by *Sam. Argal* of *Walthamstow* in *Essex*, Doctor in Physick, *Candidat & Honerary* and *Physitian* in Ordinary to Her Majesty.

Argal.

9. *Per Fess* Sable and Argent, a *Lyon Rampant* Counterchanged by the Name of *Vaugham*, and is born by the Right Honourable *Richard* Earl of *Carbury* in *Ireland*, and Baron of *Emlyn* in *England*.

Earl of Carbury.

10. *Per Pale Nebule* Azure and Or, six *Martlets* Counterchanged by the Name of *Fleetwood*.

Fleetwood

11. *Per Fess* Argent and Gules, a *Bar* between three Crescents Counterchanged.

12. *Paly* of six Argent and Gules, a *Bend Paly* of as many *Counterchanged.*

13, *Paly Bendy* or and Sable.

14. *Barry* of six *Indented* the one into the other Argent and Sable, by the Name of *Gill.*

Gill.

15. *Barry Bendy* Argent and Vert.

16. *Checky* Topaz and Saphir, a *Fess* Ruby, *fretty* Pearl, born by the Right

Honou-

Honourable *Charles* Lord *Cheyne*, Vif- Lord
Cheyne.
count of *Newhaven* in *Scotland*, &c.
which faid Dignity, upon the Death of
his *Lordſhip*, defcends on his Son and
Heir *William Cheyne* Efq.

17. *Checky* Argent and Gules, a Chief Mickle-
thwait.
Indented Azure, born by *Joſeph Mickle-*
thwaite of *Swayle* in *Holderneſs* in *York-*
ſhire, Efq.

18. *Checky* Or and Gules, on a *Feſs* Baldock.
Azure, three *Eſcallops* Argent, born by
Sir *Robert Baldock* of *Talconeſton* in *Nor-*
folk, Knight.

19. *Barry* of fix Parted *per Pale In-* Peyto.
dented Argent and Gules, Counterchanged, born by *William Peyto* of *Cheſterton*
in *Warwickſhire*, Efq.

20. *Barry Pily* of eight pieces, Or
and Gules.

Thus much of *Coat Armours* that have
an obfcure derivation from fome of the
Ordinaries, and do keep their Name. I
fhall next proceed to fome Examples
where two or more *Ordinaries* are joyned in one *Shield*, and which are Subject
to a Charge.

E 3   *Example*

Examples of
ORDINARIES
Joyned together.

1. **G**Ules on a *Cheveron* Argent, three Bars *Gemelle* Sable, born by Sir *Barnham Throgmorton* of *Clower-wall* in *Glocestershire*, Knight and Baronet.

Throgmorton.

2. Sable, a *Pile* Argent *Surmounted* of a *Cheveron* Gules, by the Name of *Dixon*.

Dixon.

3. Argent on a *Pile* Azure, a *Cheveron* Counterchanged Argent, and Sable, born by Sir *John Otway* of *Igmire*, in the West riding of *York-shire*, Knight, *Chancellor* of *Durham*, Vice *Chamberlain* of the County *Palatine* of *Lancaster*, and one of his Majesties *Councel* learned in the Law.

Otway.

4. Argent, two *Barrs* Gules, on a *Canton* of the second, a *Cross* of the first, born

Ordinaries

Joyned together.

born by *Thomas Broughton* of *Broughton* Brough-
in *Staffordshire* Esq; Son and Heir of Sir ton.
Bryan Broughton, Knight and Baronet.

5. Sable on a *Saltier Engrailed* Argent,
an *Escocheon* Or, charged with a *Cross*
Gules, by the Name of *Morris.*   Morris.

6. Or, a *Fess* between two *Cheverons*
Sable, born by *John Lisle* of *Moxhul* in Lisle.
Warwick-shire, Esquire.

7. Gules, two *Bars* and a *Chief Indented* Or, born by Sir *Thomas Hare* of *Stow-* Hare.
Bardolph in *Norfolk,* Baronet.

8. Argent a *Cheveron* and *Chief* A-
zure.

9. *Paly* of six Argent and Gules, a
Cheveron Or, born by Sir *Edward Bark-* B aikha.
ham of *West Acre* in *Norfolk,* Baronet.

10. *Barry* of six peices Or and Azure,
a *Bend* Gules, by the Name of *Gaunt.*   Gaunt.

11. Argent a *Pale* and *Chief* Gules.

12. Gules a *Saltier Engrailed* Argent,
and a *Chief Vairy.*

13. *Checky* Or and Azure, a Fess
Gules, born by the Right Honourable
Hugh Lord *Clifford,* Baron of *Chudleigh* Clifford.
in *Devonshire,* Son and Heir of the Right
Honourable *Thomas* Lord *Clifford* deceased, late Lord *High Treasurer* of *England,*
&c,   E 4   14. *Per*

14. *Per Pale* Argent and Vert, a *Cheveron* Engrailed Counterchanged.

B.uce.

15. Topaz, a *Saltier* and *Chief* Ruby on a *Caxton* Pearl, a *Lyon Rampant* Saphir; born by the Right Honourable *Robert Bruce*, Earl of *Ailesbury* and *Elgin*, Viscount *Bruce* of *Ampthil*, Baron *Bruce* of *Whorltone*, *Skelton* and *Kinloss*, Lord Lieutenant of the Counties of *Bedford* and *Huntington*, and one of the Lords of his Majesties most Honourable *Privy Councel*, &c.

16. Sable, a *Cheveron* within a *Bordure* Engrailed Argent.

17. *Barry* of six Or and Sable, an *Escocheon*, Argent.

18. Gyrony of four Or and Gules, a *Saltier Engrailed* Ermine.

19. *Barry* of six Argent and Gules, a *Pale* Ermine.

Elwes.

20. Or a *Fess* Azure surmounted by a *Bend* Gules, born by Sir *Gervas Elwes* of *Stoke juxta Clare* in *Suffolk* Baronet, and by Sir *John Elwes* of *Grovehouse* in the Parish of *Fulham* in *Middlesex*, Knight.

Isham.

21. Gules, a *Fess* and three *Piles* in Chiefe Wavey Argent, born by Sir *Justinian Isham* of *Lamport* in *Northampton shire*, Baronet.

22. Quar-

22. Quarterly Topaz and Ruby, a *Bend Vairy*, born by the Right Honou-rable *Charles Sackvile* Earl of *Dorset* and *Middlesex*, Baron *Bruckhurst* and *Cranfield*, one of the Gentlemen of his *Majesties Bed Chamber*, and Lord Leiutenant of *Sussex*, &c. *Earl of Dorset. Sackvile.*

This Coat is also born by Collonel *Thomas Sackvile* of *Selscombe* in *Sussex*, Son of Sir *Thomas Sackvile* of the said place, Knight of the *Bath*.

23. *Quarterly* Or and Gules a *Bend* Sable, born by Sir *James Clavering* of *Anwel* in the *Bishoprick* of *Durham*, Baronet. *Clavering*

Quarterly Argent and Gules, a *Bend* Sable, born by *Tho. Widrington* of *Finton* ham in *Northumberland* Esquire. *Widrington.*

Quarterly Sable and Or a *Bend* Argent, born by *George Laughton* of *Laugton* in *Lincolnshire* Esquire. *Laughton*

24. Argent a *Cross* Gules and *Chief* Vert.

25. Or, a *Bend* Ermine *Perforated* through a *Cheveron* Gules.

CHAP.

CHAP. III.

Treats of Coat Armour *formed of things* Artificial *, to wit, such as are made by* Man *, and for his use, which shall be reduced under several* Heads *, as they* Relate *to the use of* Civil Life *, as the* Ensigns *of* Dignity *, both* Temporal *and* Ecclesiastical *; or of* Professions *both* Liberal *and* Mechanical *, or as they* Relate *to* Military Actions *, as well for the* Land *as* Sea.

CIVIL ARTIFICIAL THINGS.

1. J*Upiter* a *Scepter Royal* in *Pale*, insigned with an *Eye Sol.*
   The *Eye* betokeneth Providence in Government, being the *Watchman* of the Body, and the *Scepter* is an Emblem of Justice.   2. *Luna*

Civill Artificiall
things.

2. *Luna* a *Mound,Saturn* environed with a *Circle*, and ensigned with a *Cross Evallane Mars.*

This as *Guillim* notes, is an *Ensign* Representing Soveraign *Majesty and Jurisdiction* of a King, and therefore it is blazoned by the *Planets.*

By the roundness of the *Mound*, and insigning thereof with a *Cross*, is signifyed, that *Religion* and the Faith of *Christ* ought to be received and embraced throughout his *Dominions.*

3. *Sol*, a *Cap* of *Maintenance Mars* turned up Ermine.

This is called a *Cap* of *Maintenance*, for that Pope *Julius* the second sent such an one with a Sword to King *Henry* the eighth, for he had lately before that written a Book against *Martin Luther*; and after that, Pope *Leo* the Tenth gave him the Title of *Defender of the Faith*

4. *Luna*, a *Mantle* of *Estate*, *Mars* doubled Ermine, ouched *Sol*, garnished with Strings fastned thereunto fretways dependant, and tasselled of the same.

The *Mantle* is a Robe of *Estate* peculiar to *Monarchs*, and free *Estates.*

These Arms do belong to the Town of Brecknock in *Wales.*

Town of
Brecknock.

5. *Jupiter*

5. *Jupiter*, *a Mace* of *Majesty* in *Bend Sol*.

It is called a *Mace* of Majesty to diftinguish it from a *Mace* born by a Common Sergeant.

6. Pearl three *Garters* Buckled and nowed Saphir, garnifhed with *Diamonds*.

This *Garter* is worn by the *Knights* of the *Garter*.

7. Gules three *Taffels* Or, by the Name of *Wooler*.

Wooler.

8. *Saturn* an *Imperial* Crown *Sol*.

Of *Crowns* I fhall fpeak more in the Chapter of external *Ornaments*.

9. Gules three *Ducal Crowns* Or, on a *Chiefe* of the fecond as many *Laurel Leaves* proper, born by Sir *John Berkenhead* Knight, deceafed.

Berkenhead.

10. Pearl a *Sword* of *Eftate* in *Pale*, the point erected Ruby, hilted, and pomelled Topaz; the Scaberd enriched with precious *Stones* proper.

The manner of bearing this *Sword* varieth according to the feveral *Eftates* and *Dignities* of the *Perfons* for whom they are born.

11. Or, a *Cardinals Hat* with *Strings* pendent and plated in true-love, the ends meeting in bafe Gules.

Such

Such *Red Hats* are worn by the *Cardinals* at *Rome* and other *Catholick* Countries.

12. *Venus*, a *Staff* in Pale *Sol*, and thereupon a *Cross Pattee*, *Luna* surmounted off a *Pall* of the last, charged with 4. like Crosses fitched Saturn, edged and stringed as the second. This *Coat* belongs to the *Archiepiscopal See* of *Canterbury*, to whose place it appertains to Crown and Inaugurate the Kings of *England*.

13. Vert, three *Gem Rings* Or, enriched with *Turkasses* proper.

Though Custom and Time hath made the *Ring* a common Ornament for every *Mechanick Hand*, yet of right none should use and wear them, but such as either by *Blood*, *Wars*, *Learning*, or *Office* and *Dignity* were made capable thereof.

14. Azure; a *Bishops Crosier* in Pale Erect Or. The *Crosier* was given to the *Bishops* as an Emblem to fetch and draw the Souls of men to their Lord and Master *Jesus Christ*.

15. Or, Six *Annulets* 3 2 and 1 Sable, by the Name of *Lowther*, and is born by Sir *John Lowther* of *Lowther-Hall* in *Westmoreland* Baronet.

By

By Sir *William Lowther* of *Pontefract* in the North-Riding of *Yorkshire*, Knight.

By *Anthony Lowther* of *Mask* in *Cleaveland*, in the *North Riding* of *Yorkshire*, Esq.

By *Henry Lowther* of *Cockermouth* in *Cumberland*, Esquire,

Azure six *Annulets*, 3 2 and 1 Or, born by Sir *Phillip Musgrave* of *Edenhall* in *Cumberland*, Knight and Baronet, Governour of *Carlisle* Garison.

Musgrave.　By Sir *Edward Musgrave* of *Hayton Castle* in the said County Baronet.

By Sir *Christopher Musgrave* of *Eden Hall* in the said County Knight, second Son to the said Sir *Phillip*.

By *William Musgravve* of *Musgrave Hall* in *Penrith*.

By *William Musgrave* of *Clea*, both of the said County, Esquires.

And by *Edward Musgrave* of *Ashby* in *Westmorland*, Esquire.

Goreing.　16. Argent à *Cheveron* between, three *Annulets* Gules, born by *Thomas Goreing* of *Kinston* in *Staffordshire* Esquire, and by *Lovet Goreing* of the *Inner Temple*, *London*, Gent.

The Charge of *Annulets* are born several ways, and of greater or lesser quantities, as by these examples may appear.

Ar-

Argent, three *Annulets* in *Chief* Gules.

Azure, fiue *Annulets* in Crofs Or.

Barry of fix Argent and Azure, over all three *Annulets* Or.

Per Fefs Argent and Sable, fix *Annulets Counterchanged.*

Gules on a *Chief Indented* Argent, three *Annulets* Sable.

17. Gules, ten *Billets*, 4, 3, 2 and 1. Qr, by the Name of *Cawdrey*.   Cawdrey

If the number of *Billets* be ten, or under, then in the blazoning Name, the quantity of them, but if above, then the Number is not expreft.

18. Diamond a *Bend Engrailed* between fix *Billets* Pearl, born by the Right Honourable *VVilliam* Lord *Allington*, Baron of *VVymondley* in the Kingdom of *England*, and Baron of *Killard* in *Ireland*, *Conftable* of his Majefties *Tower* of *London*.   Lord *Allington.*

19. Gules 3 *Pens* Argent.

20. Ermine 3 *VVheeles* Sable.

21. Argent, a *Crofs* Gules in the firft quarter, a *Katherin VVheel* of the fecond.

This *VVheel* differs from the plain, which is of ufe for *Carts* and other *Carriages*, it having Teeth fet round it, and was much in ufe in the primitive Age of

the

the Church for the torturing *Christians*, and took it's Name St.*Katherin*, that suffered Martyrdom on such a kind of *Wheel*.

22. Gules 3 *Katherin VVheels* Argent, on a *Chief* of the second a *Bulls head* couped Sable, born by Sir *Phillip Matthews* of *Edmonton* in *Middlesex* Baronet, and by *Joachin Mathews* of *Lincolns Inn* in *Middlesex*, Esquire.

23. Or, three *Text Esses* Sable.

24. Vert, two *Organ Pipes* in *Saltier* between four *Crosses Pattee* Argent.

It is said that *Jubal* the Son of *Lamech* was the first that found out *Musical Instruments*.

25. Azure a *Harp* Or, stringed Argent, this is the Armes of *Ireland*, quartered in his Majesties Royal Atchievement.

Ix-

Civill Artificiall
things.

Other Examples of

CIVIL ARTIFICIAL THINGS.

1. PEarl, a *Maunch* Diamond, born by *Theophilus* Earl of *Huntington*, Baron *Haſtings*, *Hungerford*, *Botreaulx*, *Moulins*, *Moules*, *Homet* and *Peverel*, **Earl of** *Huntington* and one of the Lords of his Majeſties moſt Honourable *Privy Councel*, &c.

The word *Maunch* is derived from the Latin word *Manica*, which ſignifies the *Sleeve* of a *Garment*.

2. Argent, a *Cheveron* between three *Maunches* Sable, born by Sir *Edward Mauncel* or *Mergan* in *Glamorganſhire*, **Mauncell,** Baronet.

3. Or a *Purſe Overt* Gules.

4. Gules a *Cheveron* between three *Iriſh Broges* or *Shoes*, Or.

F

5. Azure

5. Azure a *Plough* in Fes Argent, by the Name of *Kroge*.

Kroge.

6. Gules three *Scithes* in Pale Barways Argent, by the Name of *Kemple*.

Kemple.

7. Sable, a *Cheveron* between three *Tuns* Argent, born by the Company of *Vintners*.

8. Argent three *Fusils* upon *Slippers* Gules.

They are called *Fusils* from *fucus*, which signifies a Spindle of Yarn. *Pliny* faith it was a fashion and custom at *Rome*, that when *Maids* were to be Wedded, there attended upon them one with a *Distaff* with dressed Wool, as also with a Spindle and Yarn upon it, to put them in mind that *Housewifery* and *Wivery* were to go together.

9. Argent, three *Weavers Shuttles* Sable, tipped and furnished with their *Quills* of *Yarn* or *Thread* Or, born by *John Skuttleworth* of *Newby Hall* in *Yorkshire*, Gentleman.

Shuttle-
worth.

10. Argent a *Cheveron* between three Carpenter Squares Sable, by the Name of *Atlow*.

Atlow

11. Argent a *Fefs* between three pair of *Pincers* Gules.

12. Gules

12. Gules a *Cheveron* between three *Malletts* Or, born by *John Soame* of little Thurlow in *Suffolk* Esquire.

13. Or on a *Feß* Azure, three *Hawks Bells* of the first.

These sort of *Bells* are of great antiquity, being worn by the *Hebrews High-Priests* on the *Skirts* of their upper Garments, in their Divine Worship, to move the People to Attention. And the great *Bells* were invented to hang in *Churches*, to call the People to Divine Service.

14. Sable three *Bells* Argent, by the Name of *Porter*.

15. Argent three Bugle, or *Hunters Horns* Sable stringed Gules and garnished Or, born by *Alan Bellingham* of *Leaven* in *Westmoreland* Esquire.

Argent three *Bugle-hornes* Sable, stringed Vert and *Garnished* Or, is born by *Humfrey Wyrley* of *Hampstead Hall* in *Staffordshire* Esquire, one of the *Prothonotaries* of his Majesties Court of *Common Pleas*.

16. Vert, *fretty* Or, born by Sir *Will. Whitmore* of *Apley* in *Shropshire*, Baronet.

By *William Whitmore* of *Balms* in Middlesex Esquire.

Soame.

Por..r.

Bellingham.

Wyrley.

Whitmore.

Sable *Fretty* Or, born by Sir *John Bel-*

Bellew. *lew* of *Bellews Town* in the County of *Meath* in *Ireland*, Knight.

17. Gules a *Frett* Argent, born by Sir

Fleming. *Daniel Fleming* of *Ridale* in *Westmoreland* Knight, and by *Edward Fleming* of *In-flow* in *Devonshire* Esquire.

Sable a *Frett* Argent by the Name of

Haring- *Harington.*

ton.   Gules a *Frett Engrailed* Ermine, by

Eyneford. the Name of *Eyneford.*

18. Or *Fretty* Gules, a *Canton* Ermine, born by the Right Honourable *Edward Noel,* Viscount *Campden* , Baron of *Red-lington* and *Elmington,* and Earl of *Ganes-*

Earl of Ga- *borough* , Lord Leiutenant of *Rutland-*
nesborough. *shire* :

And with a due difference, is born by the *Honourable John Noel* of *Luffingham* in *Rutlandshire* Esquire, third Son of the

Noel. Right Honourable *Baptist Noel,* Viscount *Campden* , &c.

19. Argent, a *Frett* of eight peices Gules, each charged in the midst with a

Hamilden *Flower de lis* Or, by the Name of *Ha-milden.*

20. Argent *Frette* Gules *semy de Castles*

Nechur. of the second by the Name of *Nechur.*

21. Ar-

21. Argent three *Weels*, their *Hoopes* upward Vert.

22. Or three *Dice* Sable, each charged with an Ace Argent, by the Name of *Ambes Ace*.

There is no Fortune in the *Dice*, but all Ominous, for he that loofeth is tormented, and he that wineth is enticed to play on until he is enfnared, and it may be loofe far more then he formerly won, befides the ill Accidents that often attend, even to murther it felf.

23. Ermine on a Crofs quarter pierced Argent, four *Ferdemolins* Sable, born by Sir *Edmond Turner* of *Stoke Rochford* in Turner. *Lincolnfhire*, Knight.

24. Azure a *Fefs* between three *Chefs-rooks* Or, by the Name of *Bodenham*.   Bodenham

This is a thing ufed in the Play of *Chefts*, being for the defence of all the reft, and ftands in the utmoft Corner of the *Cheft Board*, or *Frontier Caftle*.

F 3   *Other*

Other Examples of

CIVIL ARTIFICIAL
THINGS.

Warcup.

1. SAble three *Cups* covered Argent, bore by *Edmond Warcup* of *North More* in *Oxfordshire*, Esq.

Butler.

2. Argent, on a *Chief* Sable, three *Cups Covered* Or, born by Sir *James Butler* of *Lincolns Inn*, Knight, *Steward* of his Majesties *Palace* and *Marshalsea Court*.

And by *Nicolas Butler* of *Hailes* in over *Rawcliff* in *Lancashire*, and of the *City* of *London*, Doctor in *Physick*.

3. Gules a *Fusil* Argent.

Earl of Clarendon.

4. Saphir, a *Cheveron* between three *Lozenges* Topaz, born by the Right Honourable *Henry* Earl of *Clarendon*, Viscount *Cornbury*, and Baron *Hide* of *Hendon*, and by the Right Honourable *Laure Hide*,

Earl

Civill Artificiall
things.

Earl of *Rochester*, firſt Lord Commiſſio- ner of his Majeſties Treaſury, and one of the Lords of his moſt Honourable Privy Councel.

5. Gules a *Maſcle* Argent.

The *Fuſil* is longer then the *Lozenge*, having its upper and lower parts more acute and ſharp then the other two cola-teral middle parts.

The *Lozenge* differs from the *Fuſil* in that it is not ſharp at the top and bottom, but all the *Lines* of an equal length.

A *Maſcle* is in form and ſhape like the *Lozenge*, but that it is voided as in the *Eſcocheon* appears.

6. Argent a *Cheveron* between 3 Fuſils Ermenois, born by Sir *John Shaw* of *El-* *tham* in *Kent*, Baronet, and by Mr *Tho-mas Shaw* of the City of *London*, Mer-chant.

7. Argent on a *Bend* Sable, three *Maſ-cles* of the Field, born by *Rowland Carle-* *ton* of *Ampthil* in *Bedfordſhire*, Gentle-man.

8. Pearl three *Lozenges* in *Feſs* Ruby, within a *Bordure* diamond, born by the Right Honourable *Charles Mountague*, Earl of *Mancheſter*, Viſcount *Mandevil*, Baron of *Kimbolton*.

 By

Earl of Sandwich.

By the Right Honourable *Edward Montague*, Earl of *Sandwich*, Viscount *Montague* of *Hinchingbrook*, and Baron of St. *Neots*.

By the Right Honourable *Edward* Lord *Montague* of *Boughton*.

By *Edward Montague* of *Horton* in *Northamtonshire* Esquire.

And by *William Montague* Esquire, Son and Heir of the Right Honourable *William Montague*, Lord Chief *Justice* of his Majesties Court of *Exchequer*.

9. Argent a *Rundle*.

The *Rundle* is a thing much used in *Coat* Armour, but by different Names, it retaining one and the same shape, and the Names appropriated to it, doth declare the *Colour* without naming it; and of these *Rundles*, there are nine sorts, (*viz.*) *Bezants* whose Colour is Or. *Plates* whose Colour is Argent. *Torteauxes*, whose Colour is Gules. *Hurts*, whose Colour is Azure. *Pellets* or *Ogresses*, whose Colour is Sable. *Pomeis* is Vert. *Golpes* is Purpure. *Oranges* is Tenne, and *Guzes* is Sanguine.

And of these three are the usual bearing either in a Field by themselves, or on, or between any of the Ordinaries, as by

the

the Examples in the *Efcocheon* doth appear.

10. Or three *Torteauxes*, born by Sir *William Courteney* of *Powderham Caftle* in *Devonfhire* Baronet.

And by *John Courteney* of *Knowftone* in the faid County, Efquire.

11. Argent, three *Torteauxes* in *Bend*, Cottized Sable by the Name of *Ince*.

12. Or, on a Fefs Sable three *Plates*, born by Sir *John Bramfton* of *Screens* in *Effex*, Knight of the *Bath*, and by *Francis Bramfton* of *Sergeant Inn London*, Sergeant at Law, Brother to the faid Sir *John*.

13. Sable, two *Bars* Argent in Chief, three *Plates*, born by Sir *Edward Hungerford* of *Farley* Caftle in *Hampfhire*, Knight of the *Bath*.

14. Argent Six *Plates*, three, two and one.

15. Or, on a *Pale* Azure, 3. *Bezants* born by *John Wildman* of *Beaucot* alias *Becket* in *Berkfhire*, Efq.

16. Argent a *Crofs* Sable between four *Pellets*, born by Sir *Robert Clayton* of the City of *London*, Knight and Alderman, late Lord Mayor thereof.

Courteney.

Ince.

Bramfton.

Hungerford.

Clayton.

17 Sable

17. Sable ten *Plates*, four, three, two and one, on a Chiefe Argent, a *Lyon Paffant* Sable, born by Sir *John Bridgman* of *Castle Bromwick* in *Warwick-shire*, Baronet, Son aud Heir of the Right Honourable Sir *Orlando Bridgman*, Knight and Baronet deceafed, late Lord *Keeper* of the Great Seal of *England*.

By *Orlando Bridgman* of *Within-Brook* in *Warwick-shire* Efquire, fecond Son of the faid Sir *Orlando*.

And by *William Bridgman* of *York=buildings* in the Parifh of St. *Martins* in the *Fields* in *Middlefex* Efquire.

18. Gules on a *Cheveron* Or three *Croffes Forme Fitche* Sable, between as many *Bezants*, born by *Erafmus Smith* alias *Herez* of St. *Jones* in the Parifh of *Clarkenwel* in *Middlefex* Efquire, Son of Sir *Roger Smith* of *Edmonthorp* in *Leicefter-shire*, Knight, deceafed.

19. Argent, three *Bars* Sable in *Chiefe*, as many *Torteauxes*, all within a *Bordure* Ermine, born by Sir *Thomas Bludworth* of *Leather head* in *Surrey* Knight, Son and Heir to Sir *Thomas Bludworth* of the faid place, and of the City of *London*, Knight, Alderman and Lord Mayor, *Anno* 1666.

Hav-

Bridgman

Smith.

Bludworth

Military things.

Having treated of *CIVIL ARTIFICI-AL THINGS*, next comes in Order *Military things* as well for Offence as Defence.

Examples of

MILITARY THINGS.

1. **A**Rgent a *Tower tripple Tower'd* Gules, chained Tranfverfe the Port Or.

Caftles and *Towers* are places of ftrength, and commonly feated on a lofty Affent, and in places of ftrength both by Nature and Art, and do ferve for places of re-fuge and retreat, rather then for the va-lorous to perform any Noble exploit in, and many times *Caftles* and *Towers* have proved very pernitious to thofe that have repofed truft in their fafety.

2. Or a *Tower* Sable, having a *Scaling Ladder* raifed againft it in *Bend Sinifter* Argent. 3. Ar-

3. Argent a *Tower tripple Tower'd* Sable, on a *Mount* proper, born by Sir Richard *Chiverton* of *London* Knight and Alderman.

4. Or a *Castle tripple Tower* Gules, the *Ports* Displayed of the Field, leaved Argent.

Mr. *Guillim* obſerveth that when the *Architecture* or *Maſonry* extendeth all over the Field, from one ſide to the other, it muſt be blazoned a *Caſtle*.

5. Argent a *Bridge* of three *Arches* in *Feſs* Gules maſoned Sable, the ſtreams transfluent proper, a *Fane* Argent, by the Name of *Trowbridge*.

6. Sable a *Cheveron* between three *Tents* Argent, by the Name of *Tenton*.

Tents and *Tabernacles* were the Chiefe Habitation of our Fore-Fathers, and ſuch kind of Habitations were beſt for their convenience for the often removing their Seat, for the refreſhing their *Cattle* with change of *Paſtures*. And this *Cuſtom* is at this day obſerved by the *Tartarians*, and ſome other of the Eaſtern People:

7. Gules three *Single Arches* Argent, the *Capitals* and *Pedeſtals* Or.

8. Azure three *Banners* diſvelloped, or diſplayed in *Bend* Or.

Ban-

Banners are very useful for every *Band* of Foot, or Troop of *Horse* to gather their Company together, each *Banner* having some particular mark of diftinction for their better knowledge thereof.

9. Ermine a *Crofs Bow* bend in *Pale* Gules, by the Name of *Arblafter*.

Arblafter.

The *Crofs Bow* is faid to be firft devifed by the *Grecians*.

10. Gules a *Cheveron Engrailed* between three *Trumpets* Argent.

The *Trumpet* was made by the immediate direction and command of *God* to *Mofes*, and was to be ufed for the affembly of the Congregation, and for the departure of the *Camp*. And the found of the *Trumpet* is but as the loud voice of the *General*, and although the *Trumpeter* fights not, yet his founding doth much excite and encourage the *Soldiers* to valour.

11. Gules a *Drum* in *Fefs* between three *Drumfticks* erected Argent.

This loud founding *Inftrument* is of like ufe with the *Trumpet*, and ufed by many Nations.

Zizca that renowned Captain of the *Bohemians* being fick to Death, defired his *Souldiers*, when he was dead, to flea him

him, and make a *Drum* of his Skin, af-
nring them that when their Enemies
should hear the sound thereof they
would put them to flight.

12. Sable, a *Beacon* fired Or, the flame
proper.

Upon the Invasion of an Enemy the
Beacons are set on fire, which presently
gives an Alarum to the whole *Country*,
and such *Beacons* are placed upon high
Hills, as in *Kent*, *Essex*, and other Frontier Counties of *England*, for the like occasion when need requires.

13. Argent a *Culvering* dismounted in
Fess Sable, by the Name of *Leigh*.

14. Azure three *Murthering Chain shots*
Or.

15. Pearl three *Battering Rams* barways proper, *headed* Saphir, Armed and
Garnished Topaz, by the Name of *Bertie*, and is born by the Right Honourable
Robert Earl of *Lindsey*, Baron *Willoughby*
of *Eresby*, Lord Great *Chamberlain* of
England, Lord Leiutenant of *Lincolnshire*, and one of the Lords of his Majesties most Honourable Privy Councel, *&c.*

Also by his Lordships Brother the
Right Honourable *James* Lord *Bertie*,
Barron *Norris* of *Rycot*, Earl of *Abing-
ton*

ton, and Lord Leiutenant of *Oxford-shire*.

This Coat with a due difference, is born by the Honourable Captain *Peregrin Bertie* of *Waldershire* in *Kent*.

By the Honourable Captain *Richard Bertie* of *Creton* in *Lincolnshire*. And by the Honourable Captain *Charles Bertie* of *Uffington* in *Lincolnshire*, Brothers of the Right Honourable *Robert* Earl of *Lindsey* aforesaid.

The *Battering Ram* was an Instrument much used by the *Romans* at their besieging *Cities*, or holds with purpose to surprize them; and such an *Engine* did *Titus Vespatianus* Erect against *Jerusalem*, when he took it.

16. Azure three *Launces* in *Bend* Or.

Guillim observes that it was the custom of the *Romans*, before they waged War, after a denial of restitution of things unjustly taken, or Satisfaction for injuries offered, that their *King* at *Armes* should amongst other Ceremonies throw a *Spear* headed with Iron, and imbrued with blood, and scorched with fire into the soyl of that People, against whom they intended *Wars*, to declare to them that they would with Fire and Force severely

verely punish them for injuries done them.

17. Ruby three *Clarions* Topaz, born by the Right Honourable *John* Earl of *Bath*, Viscount *Greenvile* of *Landsdown*, Baron *Greenvile* of *Kilhampton* and *Bidiford*, Lord Leiutenant of *Cornwal*, Governour of *Plimouth*, Lord Warden of the *Stanneries*, Steward of the Dutchy, *Groom* of the *Stool*, first Gent. of his *Majesties* Bed Chamber, and one of the Lords of his *Majesties* most Honourable *Privy Councel*, &c.

Earl of Bath.

The *Clarion* by some is said to be a rest for *Launces*, and by others a *Musical Instrument* used in *Battle* and *Turnaments* like unto *Trumpets*, for in many old descriptions of *Tiltings*, we find *Knights* to come in with *Clarions*.

Shipstow.

18. Sable three *Scaling Ladders* in *Bend* Argent, by the Name of *Shipstow*.

Magnal.

19. Argent a *Sweep* Azure, charged with a Ston Or, by the Name of *Magnal*.

This Instrument was used to cast *Stones* into the *Towns*, or *Fortifications* of the *Enemies*.

Military things.

Other Examples of

MILITARY THINGS.

1. ERmine three *Long Bowes* in *Pale Bent* Gules, by the Name of *Bowes*. Bowes.

2. Gules three *Arrows* Or, *feathered* and *headed* Argent, born by Sir *Edward Hales* of *Tunftal* in *Kent*, Baronet.

By Sir *Robert Hales* of *Beakesborn* in Hales, the faid County Baronet.

And by Sir *John Hales* of *Coventry* in *Warwick-fhire* Baronet.

3. Sable a *Cheveron Engrailed* between three *Arrows* Argent, born by Sir *Humfrey Fofter* of *Aldermafton* in *Bark-fhire*, Fofter. Baronet.

4. Saphir a *Crofs* between 4 *Pheons* Topaz, born by the Right Honourable *Richard Jones* Vifcount and Earl of *Rane-* Earl of *laugh*. Ranelaugh.

G

5. Vert

5. Vert on a *Cheveron* Argent, three *barbed Arrow-head* Sable, born by Sir *Charles Keymis* of *Kæven Mabley* in *Glamorgan-ſhire*, Baronet.

Keymis.

The *Bow* and *Arrows* were *Military Inſtruments*, much uſed in former Ages, before the Invention of *Guns* by the *Engliſh*, and great Execution was done thereby. And it was the cuſtom of the *Perſians* when they went to war, for every one to put an *Arrow* into a Cheſt for that purpoſe, placed before the Throne of their *King*, and at their return, for every one to take forth an Arrow, and by thoſe remaining, the number of the ſlain did the better appear.

6. Argent three *Spears heads* Gules, a *Chiefe* Azure by the Name of *Reyce*.

Reyce.

7. Sable a *Cheveron* between three *Spears heads* Argent, the points embrewed proper by the Name of *Morgan*.

Morgan.

8. Argent a *Sword* erected in Pale Sable, by the Name *de Dymock*.

Dymock.

The *Sword* is a Weapon fitted for Execution, and hath been uſed in all Ages.

9. Gules three *Swords* conjoyned at the *Pomels* in Feſs, their points extended into the *Corners* of the *Eſcochœon* Argent, by the Name of *Stapleton*.

Stapleton.

10. Azure

10. Azure three *Swords*, one in *Pale* with the Point upwards, Surmounted of the other two, placed *Saltier* ways, with the points downwards Argent, by the Name of *Norton*.   Norton.

11. Sable three *Swords*, *one* in *Pale*, *two* with their points downwards, and the middlemoſt upwards Argent by the Name of *Rawlins*.   Rawlins.

12. Gules three *Swords Barways* Argent, the *Hilts* and *Pomels* Or, born by *Chaloner Chute* of the *Vine* in *Hampſhire*, Eſquire.   Chute.

13. Diamond, three *Swords* with their *Points* downwards, meeting in the middle baſe point Pearl hilted Topaz, born by the Right Honourable Charles Earl of *Wiltſhire*, Son and Heir to the moſt Honourable *Charles* Marqueſs of *Wincheſter*, Earl of *Wiltſhire*, and Baron St. *John* of *Baſing*, &c.   Earl of Wiltſhire.

14. Azure a *Curtelaſſe* in *Bend* Argent garniſhed Or, by the Name of *Tatnal*.   Tatnal.

15. Sable three *Battle Axes* Argent, born by *John Hall* of *Bradford* in *Wiltſhire*, Eſquire.   Hall.

16. Argent a *Galley* under full Sayl Azure.

     The

The first *Ship* that we read of was made by *Noah*, for the preservation and increase of all living Creatures in the time of the *Deluge*, to wit the *Ark*, but *Jason* first made the *Galley*, which *Sesostris* King of *Egypt* used after him.

17. Azure three Peices of *Masts* Couped with their tops Argent.

18. Gules, a *Ruther* or *Helm* of a *Ship* Argent.

Cavel.   19. Vert three *Sails* Argent, by the Name of *Cavel*.

20. Gules, an *Anchor* in *Pale* Argent, the *Timber* or Cross peice Or, by the *Goodreed* Name of *Goodreed*.

The *Anchor* signifies succour in extremity.

Military things.

Other Examples of

MILITARY THINGS.

1. ARgent three *Efcocheons* or *Shields* Sable by the Name of *Lowdham*. Lowdham.

2. Or three *Efcocheons* barry of fix Verry and Gules, by the Name of *Moun-chenfey*. Moun-chenfey.

3. Argent a clofe *Helmet* Gules, gar-nifhed Or, by the Name of *Kingfley*. Kingfley.

It was the cuftom of the *Romans* in their *Wars*, to cover the *Head* peices of their light harneffed *Soldiers*, whether Horfe or Foot, with the skins of *Bears*; and the *Grecians* ufed to cover their *Heads* with the skins of *Otters*, inftead of *Hel-mets*, and both to the end that they fhould appear more terrible and gafhly to their Enemies, and by fuch a furprize they might the better gain the Victory.

G 3   4. Azure

4. Azure two *Bars* Argent, between three *Close Helmets* Or, born by *Gabriel Armiger* of *North Creake* in *Norfolk*, and of the *Inner Temple London*, Esquire.

Armiger.

5. Argent, three *Helmets* with their *Bevers* open Sable, by the Name of *Miniet*.

Miniet.

6. Azure a *Morion* proper. This is the *Morion* now in use for the Foot *Soldiers*.

7. Pearl a *Cheveron* Ruby between three *Morions* or *Steel Caps* Saphir, born by the Right Honourable *Francis* Lord *Brudenel*, Son and Heir to the Right Honourable *Robert* Earl of *Cardigan*, Baron *Brudnel* of *Stonton*, &c.

Brudenel.

8. Saphir three left hand *Gauntlets* Topaz, born by the Right Honourable *Charles Fane* Earl of *Westmoreland*, Baron *de Spencer* and *Burgwash*, whose second Son is the Honourable Sir *Francis Fane* of *Fulbeck* in *Westmoreland* Knight of the *Bath*.

Fane.

9. Gules three *Dexter Arms Vambraced* proper, by the Name of *Armstrong*.

Armstrong.

10. Argent on a *Pile* Azure, three *Dexter Gauntlets* of the Field, born by *Thomas Jolliff* of *Costen Hall* in *Worcestershire*

Jolliff.

shire Esquire, and by *William Jolliff* of *Craswel Castle* in *Staffordshire*, Esq.

11. Ruby three *Legs* Armed proper, conjoyned in *Fess* at the upper part of the Thigh flexed in triangle, garnished and spotted Topaz. This is the Arms of the Isle of *Man*, and is quartered by the Right Honourable the Earl of *Derby*.

12. Vert a *Bar Company* Argent and Azure, between three *Curasses*, or *Brest-Plates* of Armour of the second, on a *Chiefe* of the same, as many *Fermailes* or *Buckles*, as the third by the Name of *Baldberny* of *Scotland*.

13. Argent three *Saddles* with *Stirrups* Gules.

14. Or, three *Chaplets* Vert, by the Name of *Richardson*.

Guillim observeth that *Chaplets* were by the *Romans*, given as a *Reward* of Honour for some *Military Services* performed, and they were of several sorts, some were made of *Lawrel*, others of *Oaken Leaves*, *Palme*, *Ivy*, *Olive*, and some of *Gold*, and some of *Silver*, also some of *Roses*, *Violets* and such like *Flowers*.

15. Argent on a *Cheveron* Sable, five *Horseshoes* Or, born by Sir *Nicholas Crispe* of *Hamersmith* in *Middlesex*, Baronet.

 16. Ar-

16. Argent, a *Shackbolt* Sable, by the Name of *Newthal*.

17. Gules, three *Waterbougets* Argent, by the Name of *Roos*.

18. Gules, a *Fess* between three *Waterbougets* Ermine, born by Sir *Thomas Meers* of *Lincoln* Knight, one of the *Commissioners* of the *Admiralty*.

19. Argent, three *Waterbougets* Azure.

This kind of *Waterbouget* was antiently used in *Cout Armour*.

20. Vert, a *Chevalier* Armed at all points *a Cape a pee* Brandishing his *Sword* aloft Argent, garnished Or, mounted on a Barded Courser, furnished throughout as the second, garnished as the third.

CHAP.

CHAP. IV.

Treats of Common Charges *in* Coat Armour *whereof some are* Natural, *and meerly* formal *as* Angels, *and* Spirits, *and others both* formal *and* material *as the* Sun, Moon, *and* Stars, *as also such* Natures *as are* sublinar, *as all kinds of* Minerals *which have Life after a sort as* Vegetables, *and* Sensitive Creatures *which have perfect Life.*

COmmon Charges are *things Natural,* or *Artificial*; those *Artificial* are already handled. Things Natural are Formal, or Material, and are of that great variety that it can't be expected in so small a Volumn to pass through all the particulars of them, but only give some examples that may serve to instruct the *Reader* to Blazon a Coat of the like charge.

C*s*-

Celestials are born single, or upon, or between any of the *Honourable Ordinaries,* and then three are the usual number.

Examples of

CELESTIALS.

1. **M**ars an Angel standing direct with his hands conjoyned and elevated upon his breast habited in a long Robe close girt *Luna.* his Wings displayed as prepared to fly *Sol.*

Angels are incorporeal Essences of a Spiritual Nature void of all material substances. They are the *Messengers* by whom God hath manifested his Will and Power to his Elect, and in Scripture they are said to be ministring Spirits.

2. *Luna,* on a chief *Jupiter* a *Cherub* displayed *Sol.*

The *Cherubins* were drawn with Wings before the place where the *Israelites* prayed
ed

Cælestialls.

ed manifesting the great speed when they went about the Lords business.

3. Or a *Sphere* Azure beautified, and replenished with variety of Celestial Bodies encompassing the *Terrestrial Globe* all proper.

These were the Ornaments wherewith the shield of *Achilles* was garnished.

4. Azure a *Star* of sixteen points Argent born by *John Huitson* of *Cleasby* in *Yorkshire* Esquire, one of the Captains of his *Majesties Companie* of Foot Guards.

5. Sable a *Fess Wavey* between the *Pole Stars Artick* and *Artartick* Argent, born by Sir *Francis Drake* of *Buckland Mona-* Drake. *chorum* in *Devonshire Bar* ! Descendant of the famous Sir *Francis Drake* Knight that sailed about the World, making great discoveries thereof.

A *Star* commonly consists of six *Points,* or *Raies,* and then in the Blazoning the number needs not be exprest ; but if of more, then name of what number as in the former examples.

Stars were Created by God to give light, and with their influences to be assistant to the *Sun* and *Moon* in the *Procreation, Production,* and *Fructification* of *Seeds Plants* and *Herbs* ; as also for the designation

nation and foreshewing of Times and
Seasons as the *Sun* and *Moon* were.

Stars are sometime peirced, and other
whiles charged, and when peirced the peircing is round.

6. Pearl, a *Cheveron* between three
Stars Diamond, born by the Right Honourable *Charles* Lord Viscount *Mordaunt* Lord *Mor-*
daunt. of *Aveland*, and Baron of *Rygate*.

7. Saphir, three *Stars* and a *Chief Wavey*
Topaz born by the Right Honourable
Charles Bodvel, Viscount *Bodmyn* Grand- Lord *Bod-*
myn. son and Heir to the Right Honourable
John Lord *Robarts*, Baron of *Truro*, Viscount *Bodmyn*, Earl of *Radnor*, and Lord
President of His *Majesties* most Honourable Privy Counsel.   And is also born by
the Honourable *Hender*, and *Francis Ro-* *Robarts.*
barts Esquires, Sons of the Right Honourable *John* Earl of *Radnor*, &c.

8. Gules, a *Blazing Star*, or *Comet*
streaming in *Bend* proper.

The *Comets* have been observed to
Prognosticate dreadful events of things
to come, as *Pestilence*, *Famine*, *War* and
the like.

Sometimes the stream is born upwards
as it was before the great Pestilence in
1665, but most commonly it is born
downwards.   9. Argent

9. Argent, a *Cheveron* Sable between three *Flames* of Fire proper.

Fire in the *Scripture* is oft times taken for a special token of Gods favour, and that he is pleased with the Sacrifices that are done unto him, and Fire betokeneth zeal. Some Writers affirm that none of the *Mechanical Trades* were found out before they had Fire; but afterwards daily was put in practice some new invention or other, yet as it is a good Servant so it is (as also Water) a bad Master.

10. Azure, a *Crefcent* encircled within an *Orl of Stars* Or, a *Border* of the Second, born by *Thomas Burton* of *London* Esquire. **Burton.**

11. Azure a *Sun* in his Glory, by the name of Saint *Clere*. **St. Clere.**

The *Sun* is a glorious Body, the Fountain of Light, and the production of *Fruits*, *Plants*, and all the Splendor that the *Moon* hath she borroweth from him, and between both these there is a great conformity.

12. Gules a *Chief* Argent on the lower part thereof a *Cloud*, the *Suns* resplendent Raies issuing thereout proper, by the name of *Lefone*. **Lefone.**

13. Azure one *Raye* of the *Sun* issuing

ing out of the dexter corner of the *Esco-*
cheon Bendwayes proper by the name of
Aldam.

Aldam.

14. Or a *Sun* Eclipsed Sable.

The *Suns Eclipse* is occasioned by the interposition of the *Moon* betwixt it and
the Earth.

Descus.

15. Gules an *Increscent* Or by the name
of *Descus*.

This is the State of the *Moon* from
her entrance into her first quarter, in
which time she is more and more illumi-
nated until she hath filled her Circle.

16. Gules, a *Moon* in her Complement
Or Illustrated with all her Light proper
which is sufficient without naming the
colour which is Argent.

The *Moon* is the *Mistress* by which all
moist, mutable, and inconstant things are
ruled, as a *Woman*, the *Sea*, *Rivers*, and
Fountains The Ebbing and Flowing of
the Sea following the *Moons* motion.

De la Luna.

17. Azure, a *Moon decressent* proper, by
the name of *De la Luna*.

This is the state of the *Moon* in her
Wain, the Horns must always be turned
towards the left hand of the *Escocheon*,
as that in her *Complement* is towards the
right.

Ar-

18. Argent, a *Moon* in her detriment or *Eclipse* Sable.

The *Moon* is eclipsed always in her full State, and is so occasioned by the interposition of the Earth betwixt her and the Sun.

Lucy.

19. Azure, a **Crescent** Argent, born by *Jacob Lucy* of *London* Esquire.

Rider.

20. Azure, three *Crescents* Or, born by *Robert Rither*, or *Rider* of *Scarcraft* in *Yorkshire* Esquire. And by *Thomas* and *William Rider* of *Bednal Green* in *Middlesex* Esquire.

Sable, three *Crescents* Argent by the name of *Gleve.*

Gleve.

Gules, three *Crescents* Argent by the name of *Perpoint.*

Perpoint.

Gules, the *Crescents* Ermine by the name of *Fleming.*

Fleming.

Gules, three *Crescents* Or, by the name of *Monnings.*

Monnings.

21. Pearl, a *Fess* between three *Crescents* Diamond born by the Right Honourable *Edward Henry Lee* Earl of *Litchfield*, Viscount, *Quarenton*, and Baron *Spilsbury.*

Earl of *Litchfield.*

22. Diamond, a *Fese* Ermine between three *Crescents Topaz*, born by the Right Honourable

Coventry.

Honourable *George Coventry* Baron of *Aiesborough* in *Worcestershire*, &c.

And by the Honourable *Henry Coventry* Esquire, Son to the Right Honourable *Thomas* Lord *Coventry* Lord Keeper of the great *Seal* of *England*.

Weld.   23. Azure, a *Fess Nebule* between three *Crescents* Ermine born by *Hum, Weld* of *Lulworth Castle* in *Dorsetshire* Esquire Governour of His Majesties Isle and Castle of *Portland*, and *Sandes Foot*.

24. Gules, a *Star* issuing from between the Horns of a *Crescent* Argent.

Other Examples of
Crescents.

OR on a *Chief Indented* Sable, three *Crescents* Argent, by the name of
Harvey.   *Harvey*.

Sable, a *Cross engrailed* between four *Crescents* Argent by the name of *Barnham*.

Barnham.   *Per Pale* Sable and Argent, three *Crescents* counter-changed by the name of
Topcliff.   *Topcliff*.

Barry

Cælestialls.

Barry of fix Ermine and Gules, three *Crefcents* Sable, by the Name of *Watter-ton.*

Watter-ton.

Or, five *Crefcents*, one, three, one, by the Name of *Hamond* of *Hampfhire.*

Hamond.

Argent fix *Crefcents*, three, two, one Sable, by the Name of *Blare.*

Blare.

Per *Pale* Argent and Sable, fix *Crefcents* Counterchanged by the Name of *Wickhalfe* of *Devonfhire.*

Wick-halfe.

Other Examples of

CELESTIALS.

1. ERmine, a *Mullet* of fix *Points* pierced Gules, by the Name of *Huffenhul.*

Huffenhul

Meteors are an imperfect kind of mixture engendered in the Airy Region of a certain attracted fume drawn up by the operation of the Sun and Stars, and is of a hot quality, which at length breaks into *Fire*, and so looseth or wasteth it self, and such are *Mullets* or *Flaming Stars*.

Antiently *Mullets* were born of six Points, as in this Example, but now usually of five.

2. Per *Cheveron* Or and Vert, three *Mullets* Connterchanged by the Name of *Hothe*.

Hothe.

3. Sable six Mullets, three, two, one Argent, by the Name of *Bonvile*.

Bonvile.

Azure, six *Mullets*, three, two, one Or, by the Name of *Welsh*.

Welsh.

4. Gules, on a *Chiefe* Argent, two Mullets Sable, born by Sir *Edmond Bacon* of *Redgrave Hall* in *Suffolk* Baronet.

Bacon.

By Sir *Henry Bacon* of *Lounde* in *Lovingland* in *Suffolk* Baronet.

By Sir *Nicolas Bacon* of *Shrubland Hall* in *Codenham* in the said County, Knight of the *Bath*.

Pearl on a *Chiefe* Ruby, 2 *Mullets* pierced Topaz, born by the Right Honourable *Oliver Saint John* Earl of *Bullingbrook*, &c.

Earl of Bullingbrook.

St. John:

And by Sir *Walter Saint John* of *Lydiard Tregos* in *Wiltshire*, and of *Battersey* in *Surrey* Baronet.

5. Azure

5. Azure on a *Cross* Argent, five *Mul-*
lets Gules born by Sir *Ralph Verney* of Verney.
Middle - Claydon in *Buckingham-shire* ,
Knight and Baronet.

6. Argent two *Barrs* between three
Mullet of six points pierced Sable, born
by *Phillip Dougty* of *York Buildings* in the Doughty.
Parish of St. *Martins* in the Fields in
Middlesex Esquire.

7. Per *Bend* Argent and Sable, three
Mullets of six points in *Bend* Counterchanged.

8. Argent, three *Mullets* pierced Sable, by the Name of *Wollaston*. Wollaston

Azure, three *Mullets* pierced Or, by Whit-
the Name of *Whittington* of *Lincolnshire*. tington.

Azure, three *Mullets* Or, by the Name
of *Grundin*. Grundin.

Or, three *Mullets* Sable, by the Name
of *Pelton*. Pelton.

Sable, three *Mullets* Argent, by the
Name of *Puliston*. Puliston.

Gules, three *Mullets* Argent, by the
Name of *Hansard* of *Lincolnshire*. Hansard.

9. Sable, on a *Bend* Argent, three
Mullets Gules , born by *Francis Glisson*, Glisson.
Doctor in *Physick*.

10. Azure, a *Cheveron* between three
Chetwynd   *Mullets* Or, born by *Walter Chetwynd* of
Ingestre in *Staffordshire* Esquire.

11. Or, a *Cheveron* between three
Mullets pierced Sable, born by *Thomas*
Davies.   *Davies* of *Crissing-Temple* in *Essex* Esq.
Son and Heir of Sir *Thomas Davies* of
London, Knight and Alderman decea-
sed.

12. Gules, a *Fess* between six *Mullets*
Argent, born by Sir *Denny Ashburnham*
Ashburn-   of *Broomhal* in *Sussex* Baronet, and by
ham.   *Ashburnham* of *Ashburnham* in
the said County Esquire.

13. Argent, a *Mullet* Sable, on a *Chiefe*
Gules, a *Flower de lis* Or, born by *William*
Rogers.   *Rogers* of *Castle-Hale* in the Parish of *Pans-*
wick in *Glocester-shire*.

Other

Other Examples of

Mullets.

PEr *Fes* Or and Azure, a *Mullet* of eight points Counterchanged by the Name of *Scotto*.   Scotto.

Azure, three *Mullets* and a Chiefe indented Or, by the Name of *Bright*.   Bright.

Azure, a *Crescent* between three *Mullets* Argent, by the Name of *Minshal*.   Minshal.

Per *Pale* Argent and Gules, three *Mullets*, Counterchanged by the Name of *Langford*.   Langford.

Per *Fes Indented* Gules and Or, three *Mullets* Counterchanged by the Name of *Eglington*.   Eglington.

14. Azure, *Jupiters Thunderbolt* in *Pale* Or, inflamed on both ends proper, shafted *Salterwise*, and *Winged* Fes ways Argent.

Blunt.
15. *Barre Nebule* Or and Sable, born by the Name of *Blunt.*

16. Argent, a *Rain-Bow* of divers colours proper.

Examples of

VEGETABLES:

Under which Head *all* Trees, Flowers, Plants, Leaves *and* Fruits *are or may be* comprized.

1. OR on a *Mount* in *Base*, a Pear-Tree fruited Proper, by the
Pyrton.   Name of *Pyrton.*

Argent, on a *Mount* in Base, a *Pine Ap-*
Pine.   *ple Tree* fruited, by the Name of *Pine.*

Vegetables have in them a living Power of *Growing, Budding, Leafing, Blosom-*
ing

Vegetables.

ing and *Fructifying*, as *Trees*, *Plants*, *Herbs*, *Grass*, &c. and of these, some on *Trunks* or solid Bodies, and some upon Flexible *Stocks*; some again grow upon a single *Stem*, as commonly all *Trees* do, and some upon several Stems, as *Shrubs*, *Roses*, and the like.

2. Gules, the Stem or *Trunck* of a *Tree* Eradicated, as also couped in Pale, sprouting out two Branches Argent, born by *William Burrough* of *Burrough* in *Lei-cestershire*, Gentleman.

Burrough

3. Azure a Limb of a Tree *Raguled* and Trunked in *Bend* Argent.

4. Argent, three *Stocks* or *Stumps* of Trees, couped and eradicated Sable, by the Name of *Retowre*.

Retowre.

5. Gules, three *Woodbine Leaves Pendant* Or.

The *Woodbine* is a loving and amorous Plant, embracing all that groweth near it, but without hurting of that which it loveth, and is contrary to the Ivy (which is a Type of Lust rather then Love) for it injureth that which it most embraceth.

6. Sable, three *Laurel Leaves* slipped Or.

The

The *Laurel* was in Antient times thought to be a remedy against *Poyson*, *Lightning* and the like, and in *War* used as a Token of Peace and Quietness.

7. Argent, three *Wooabine Leaves Bend ways*, two and one proper, by the Name of *Theme*.

Theme.

8. Or, three *Holly Leaves Barrways*, two and one, their Stalks towards the Dexter part of the *Escocheon* proper, by the Name of *Arneft*.

Arneft.

9. Vert, five *Figg Leaves* in *Saltier*.

10. Topaz, two *Barrs* Ruby, each charged with three *Trefoyles flipped* of the first, born by the Right Honourable *Roger Palmer* Earl of *Caftlemain*, and Baron of *Limberick* in *Ireland*.

Earl of Caftlemain

11. Azure, three *Quaterfoyls* Argent born by Sir *Anthony Vincent* of *Stoke-Dabernon* in *Surrey*, Baronet.

Vincent.

As also by *Samuel Vincent* of *Buckingham* House in *Norfolk* Esquire.

12. Argent on a *Cheveron Sable*, three *Quaterfoiles* Or, born by *N. Eyre* of *Wilton* in *Wiltfhire*, Gentleman.

Eyre.

13. Argent, three *Cinquefoils* Gules, born by Sir *Thomas Darcy* of St. *Clerrs Hall* in St. *Ofeth* in *Effex*, Baronet.

Darcy,

14. Argent

14. Argent, three *Cinquefoyls* Gules, each charged with five *Annulets* Or, born by Sir *Robert Southwel* of *Kingsweston* in *Glocestershire* Knight. Southwel.

15. Or, a *Cheveron* between three *Cinquefoyls* Gules, born by the Right Honourable Sir *Thomas Chicheley* of *Wimpley* in *Cambridgshire* Knight, Master of the *Ordinance*, and one of his Majesties most Honourable Privy Councel, *Anno* 1681. Chicheley

16. Argent on a *Chiefe* Gules, three *Cinquefoyls* of the Field, born by Sir *Thomas Bellot* of *Moreton* in *Cheshire*, Baronet. Bellet.

17. Saphir, a *Cinquefoyl* Ermine within a *Bordure* Topaz, born by the Right Honourable *Jacob* Lord *Astley*, Baron of *Reading*, &c. Lord *Astley*.

And is also the Coat of Sir *Jacob Astley* of *Melton-Constable* in *Norfolk*, Baronet.

18. Argent, a *Fess Engrailed* between three *Cinquefoyls* within a *Border* Sable, born by *Tho. Foley* of *Kidderminster* in *Worcestershire*, Esquire. By *Paul Foley* of *Stoak Court* in *Herefordshire* Esquire; and by *Phillip Foley* of *Prestwood* in *Staffordshire* Esquire, Sons of *Tho. Foley* of *Witley, of Court* in *Worcestershire*, Esq. Foley.

These

These Charges, as also *Fruits*, *Flow-ers*, &c. are born on, or between, any of the *Ordinaries*.

Examples of

FRUITS and FLOWERS.

1. A Rgent, a *Pomegranate* in *Pale slip-ped* Prope.

This *Fruit* is esteemed very good in *Physick*, whose juice is used for the allay-ing the heat of Burning or Feavorish *Agues*.

2. Azure, three *Pears* Or, by the
Stukeley. Name of *Stukeley*.

3. Gules, a *Cheveron* Ermine between three *Pine Apples* erected Or, by the Name
Pine. of *Pine*.

Under this head may be comprehend-ed all other kind of *Fruit*.

4. Azure, a *Garbe* or *Wheat-sheafe* Or,
Grosve- born by Sir *Thomas Grosvenour* of *Egton*
nour in *Cheshire*, Baronet.

Azure

Fruits, & Flowers.

Azure, a *Garb* Argent, by the Name Holdes-
of *Holdesheafe*.   heafe.

5. Sable, three *Garbs* Or, born by *Wil-*
liam Stych of *Newbury* in the Parish of Stych.
Barkin in *Essex* Esq.

Argent, three *Garbs* Sable, by the
Name of *Wanting*.   Wanting.

6. Azure, seven *Garbs* Sable, four,
two and one Or, born by Sir *Thomas*
Doleman of *Shaw* in *Bark-shire* Knight, Dolman.
one of the *Clerks* of his *Majesties* most
Honourable *Privy Councel*, Father of Sir
Humfrey Doleman, Knight.

7. Argent, on a *Cheveron* between
three *Garbs* Gules, as many *Bezants*, born
by *Tobias Eden* of the *Inner Temple*, Lon- Eden.
don, Esq.

Azure, a *Cheveron* between three *Garbs*
Or, born by the Right Honourable *Chri-*
stopher Lord *Hatton*, Governour of the Lord Hat-
Isle of *Jarsey*.   ton.

And by Mr. *Roger Hatton* of *London*,
Merchant.

8. Azure, three *Ears of Guiny Wheat*
couped and *bladed* Or, by the Name of Grand-
Grandgorge.   gorge.

9. Saphir, a *Flower de lis* Pearl, born
by the Right Honourable *George* Earl of
Bristol, Baron *Digby* of *Sherbourn*, and Bristol.
by

Ld. *Digby.* by the Right Honourable *Simon* Lord *Digby*, Baron of *Geashill* in *Ireland.*

 Or, a *Flower de lis* Azure, born by Sir
Portman. *William Portman* of *Orchard* in *Somerset-shire*, Knight of the Bath, and Baronet.

 Azure, a *Flower de lis* Or, by the Name
Stepkin. of *Stepkin.*

 Argent, a *Flower de lis* Gules, born by
Morden. *John Morden* of *London* Merchant.

 Gules, a *Flower de lis* Or, by the Name
Palford. of *Palford.*

 Gules, a *Flower de lis* Argent, by the
Walden-field. Name of *Waldenfield.*

 Vert, a *Flower de lis* Argent, by the
Fowk. Name of *Fowk.*

 10. Pearl, a *Cheveron* Ruby between three *Flower de lis* Saphir, born by the Right Honourable *Thomas* Lord Viscount
Lord Vis- *Faulconberg,* Baron of *Yarum,* Lord
countFaul- *Leiutenant* of the North Riding of *York-*
conberg. *shire,* and one of the Lords of his Majesties most Honourable Privy Councel.

 And by the Right Honourable *John*
Ld.Bellasis Lord *Belasis,* Baron of *Worlaby,* &c.

 Or, a Cheveron between three *Flower de lis* Sable, born by the Right Honoura-
Fanshaw. ble *Evelyn* Lord Viscount *Fanshaw,* his Majesties *Remembrancer* of his Court of Exchequer, &c.   By

By the Honourable *Henry Fanſhaw* of *Dengy-hall* in *Eſſex* Eſquire: And by the Honourable *Cnarles Fanſhaw* of *Dengy-hall* aforeſaid Eſquire, his Majeſties Envoy extraordinary in *Portugal*, Sons of the Right Honourable *Thomas* Lord Viſcount *Fanſhaw*, deceaſed.

11. Topaz on a *Feſs* Ruby, three *Flower de lis* of the Field, born by the Right Honourable *Thomas Leonard* Earl of *Suſſex*, and Lord *Dacres* of *Gilesland*, &c.   *Earl of Suſſex.*

Argent, on a *Feſs* Gules three *Flower de lis* Or, born by *Gervaſe Diſny* of *Norton-Deſney* in *Lincolnſhire*, Eſquire.   *Diſney.*

12. Quarterly Gules and Or, in the firſt quarter a *Flower de lis* Argent, born by *Elias Aſhmole* of the *Middle Temple*, *London* Eſquire.   *Aſhmole.*

13. Sable a *Feſs Dauncette* Or, in cheif three *Flower de lis* Argent, born by *William Feak* of *Stafford* in *Staffordſhire*, Gentleman.   *Feak.*

14. Sable, three *Lozenges* Argent, on a chief Or, as many *Flower de lis* Gules, born by Sir *Nicholas Pedley* of *Abbotſley*, and *Tetſworth* in *Huntingtonſhire*, Knight.   *Pedley.*

15. Argent, a *Cheveron* Sable, between

three

three *Columbines* flipped proper by the name of *Hall*.

Hall.

16. Sable on a *Cross* between four *Flower de lis* Argent, five *Pheons* Azure born by *Caleb Banks* of the *Friers* in *Aylesford* in *Kent* Esquire, Son and Heir of Sir *John Banks* of the said place Barronet.

Banks.

17. Or on a *Bend Engrailed* between six Roses Gules, born by *Edmond Warner* of *Warner-Hall* in *Essex* Esquire: And by *John Warner* of *Brokenthwait* in the Parish of *Kirby-overbow* in *Yorkshire* Esquire, descended from the *Warners* of *Warners-Hall* aforesaid.

Warner.

18. Gules, two *Swords* with their points erected in Saltier proper, *Hilts* and *Pomels* Or, between three *Roses* Argent, *viz.* one in *Cheif*, and two in *Fess*, born by *Patrick Trant* of Saint *Giles* in the *Fields* in *Middlesex* Esquire.

Trant.

19. Or, three *Flower de lis* Azure, a *Bordure* Gules charged with eight *Roses* Argent, born by Sir *Walter Clarges* of Saint *Martins* in the *Field* Baronet.

Clarges.

20. Sable, on a *Cheveron* Argent, three Roses Gules, seeded and Barbed proper, in the dexter cheif a *Helmet* close Bevered of the Second, born by *Robert Rose* of *Hasland* in *Derbyshire*, Gentleman.

Rose.

Un-

Under this head all other *Flowers* may be comprized; fome few more examples I have here fet down.

Argent, three Rofes Gules, by the name of *Young*. *Young.*

Gules, three *Flower de lis* Argent, by the name of *Wifemale*. *Wifemale.*

Azure, a *Vine* with *Fruit* and *Leaves* all Or.

Per Pale, Ermine and Gules, a Rofe Counter-changed, by the name of *Nightingale*. *Nightingale.*

Sable, three *Rofes* Argent, feeded Or, by the name of *Powel*. *Powel.*

Argent, fix *Rofes* 3, 2, and 1, Gules, by the name of *Palton*. *Palton.*

Argent, ten *Rofes* 4, 3, 2, 1, Gules by the name of *Payens*. *Payens.*

Gules, three *Flower de lis* Argent, by the name of *Mondeford*. *Mondeford*

Or, five *Flower de lis* 2, 1, 2, Sable by the name of *Spindelow*. *Spindelow.*

Gules, fix *Flower de lis* 3, 2, 1, Argent born by Sir *Gilbert Ireland* of *Hut*, and *Beaufie* in *Lancafhire*, Knight. *Ireland.*

Argent, three *Gilly-Flowers* proper, by the name of *Forney*. *Forney.*

From *Vegetables* as *Leaves*, *Trees*, *Plants*, *Fruits* and *Flowers*, I fhall next treat of the parts of Mans Body. *Ex-*

Examples of the

PARTS of MANS BODY.

1. JUpiter, our *blessed Lady* with her Son in her right hand, and a *Scepter* in her left all *Topaz*, this Coat belongs to the *Bishoprick* of *Salisbury*.

Bishoprick of Salisbury.

2. Gules, a *Saracens Head erazed* at the neck Argent, *environed* about the *Temples* with a wreath of the Second and Sable, by the name of *Mergith* of *Wales*.

Mergith.

3. Argent, three Blackamores Heads couped proper, banded about Gules, born by *John Tanner* of *Court* in *Cornwal* Esquire.

Tanner.

Or, three *Blackamores Heads* couped proper, banded about Argent, born by *Samuel Mico* of *London* Esquire, and by *Edward* and *Aaron Mico* of *London* Merchants.

Mico.

4. Argent,

Parts of Mans
Body.

4. Argent, a *Cheveron* Gules between three *Peruques* Sable.

Claudius furnamed *Comatus* when he gained the Government of *France* inftituted a *Law* that the *French* men fhould wear their Hair long (as his Arm was) in token of Liberty, for fhaving off the Hair was then a token of Bondage, and this was obferved by the *Romans* who ufed to fhave the Hair of their *Bondmen*.

5. Or a *Heart* proper, a cheif Sable, by the name of *Scambler*.

Scambler.

6. Argent, a *Fefs* Gules, between three *Hearts* vulned and diftilling drops of blood on the finifter fide proper, by the name of *Tote*.

Tote.

7. Azure an *Arm finifter* iffuing out of the *Dexter point* and extended towards the *finifter bafe* in form of a *Bend* Argent,

8. Vert, three *Dexter Arms* conjoined at the Shoulders and flexed in TriangleOr, with Fifts clenched Argent born by *Arthur Tremaine* of *Cullocombe* in *Devonfhire* Efquire.

Tremaia.

9. Argent, three *finifter hands couped* at the *Wrifts* and erected Gules, born by

I   Sir

Maynard. Sir *John Maynard* of *Gunnersbury* in the Parish of *Ely* in *Middlesex*, Knight, Serjeant at Law to His Majesty King *Charles* the Second.

10. Or, a *Mans* Leg couped at the midst of the thigh Azure, by the name of *Haddon.* *Haddon.*

11. Argent, a *Mans Leg* erazed at the *Prime.* *Thigh* Sable, by the name of *Prime.*

12. Ruby, three *Legs* Armed proper, conjoined in *Fess* at the upper part of the *Thigh flexed* in *Triangle*, garnished and *Arms of* spurred *Topaz,* this *Coat* is the Arms of *the Isle of* the Isle of *Man,* and is quartered by the *Man.* Earl of *Derby* as Lord of the said *Isle.*

13. Argent, *Guttee de Sang*, by the name of *Lemming.*

These *Drops* are seldom born by themselves alone, but upon or with some of the *Ordinaries.*

Gutte de Sang without naming the Colour signifies drops of Blood, and is always Gules. *Gutte de Harmes* drops of Tears which is Azure. *Gutte de Hau* drops of Water which is Argent. *Gutte de Poix,* or *Gutte de Sable*; that is drops of Pitch, and is Sable. *Gutte de* Or, drops of *Gold,* and is, Or

The form or shape of these drops are
all

all as one, only the names change the *Colours.*

14. Azure, a *Pale*, or, *Gutte de Sang*, born by Sir *Thomas Player* of *London*, *Player.* Knight, late *Chamberlain* of the said City of *London.*

15. Or, on a *Cheveron* Gules, three *dead mens Skulls*, of the field by the name of *Bolter.*   *Bolter.*

16. Sable, a *Shin-bone* in *Pale* surmounted of another in Cross Argent by the name of *Bayns.*

Of ANIMALS.

FROM the parts of *Mans Body* I shall proceed to *Animals* born in *Coat Armour* both whole and in parts, which the following Examples will demonstrate.

And of *Animals* those of prey are of most Esteem, as the *Lyon*, *Tiger*, *Bear*, *Wolf*, &c. And in Coat Armour the bearing of whole Animals being more

               worthy

worthy then the several parts, I shall first begin with them.

Of all *Creatures* apt to generation and corruption *Animals* are most worthy.

All *Savage Beasts* are naturally armed with something wherewith they may hurt their *Enemies* as the *Boar* hath *Tukes*; the *Lion Tallons*, the *Stag Horns*, the *Serpent Poyson*, and the like.

All four Footed Beasts are esteemed more worthy of bearing then *Fishes*, or *Fowls* in regard they contain in them more worthy and commendable significations of *Nobility*: and the *Males* are esteemed more worthy then the *Females*.

Examples of

BEARINGS of LIONS.

1. ARgent, a *Lion Rampant* Sable, by name of *Stapleton*.

Stapleton.

Argent, a *Lion Rampant* Gules by the name of *Verdon*.   Argent,

Verdon.

Lions.

Argent, a *Lion Rampant* vert by the name of *Springs*.

Springs.

Or a *Lion Rampant* Sable by the name of *Poley*.

Poley.

Azure, a *Lion Rampant* Or, by the name of *Beckingham*.

Beckingham

Ermine, a *Lion Rampant*. Azure, by the name of *Hardnefs* of *Kent*.

Argent, a *Lion Rampant* Sable Crowned Or, born by *Charles Morley* of *Drox-ford* in *Hantfhire* Efquire, one of the *Mafters* of *Requefts* to his Majefty King *Charles* the Second.

Morley.

Azure, a *Lion Rampant* Crowned Or, born by Sir *Francis Dayrel* of *Caftle Camps* in *Cambridgefhire* Knight.

Dayrel.

Vert, a *Lion Rampant* Or, by the name of *Morgan*.

Morgan.

Ermine, a *Lion Rampant* Azure, crowned Or, born by Sir *Henry Pickering* of *Whadden* in *Cambridgefhire* Knight, and Barronet.

Pickering.

2. Azure a *Lion Rampant Gardant* Or, born by *Fitz Hammond*.

Fitz Hammond.

Or, a *Lion Rampant Gardant* Gules, by the name of *Horon*.

Horon.

Gules, a *Lion Rampant Gardant* Or, born by *George Mafters* of *Lincolns Inn* in *Middlefex* Efquire.

Mafters.

I 3   Gules

Gules, a *Lion Rampant Gardant* Argent, by the Name of St. *Marney.*

St.*Marney,*

3. Gules, a *Lion Rampant Regardant* Or, born by *John Morice* of *London* Esq.

Morice.

Or, a *Lion Rampant Regardant* Vert, by the Name of *Hume.*

Hume.

Or, a *Lion Rampant Regardant* Gules, by the Name of *Roberts.*

Roberts.

This Action of the *Lion,* manifests an inward and degenerate Perturbation of the Mind, which is Repugnant to the generous Nature of the *Lion,* this denoting a timerous Mind, yet it betokens a diligent Circumspection, and Consideration of things to come.

4. Argent, a *Lion Rampant Coward* Purpure, by the Name of *Rowch.*

Rowch.

This Cowardly Action of claping his Tayl betwixt his Leggs (as all Beasts do that are affrighted) is contrary to the Noble Spirit of the *Lion.*

5. Or, a *Lion Rampant Double Quene* Azure, born by Sir *Christopher Wansford* of *Kirklington* in *York-shire* Baronet.

Wansford.

Or, a *Lion Rampant Double Quene* Sable, by the Name of *Wells.*

Wells.

Sable, a *Lion Rampant Double Quene* Or, by the Name of *Kingston.*

Kingston.

Azure, a *Lion Rampant Double Quene*
Or,

Or, by the Name of *Bromhall*. Bromhall.

The *Forked Tayl* is an Emblem of Magnanimity, and Strennuousness.

6. Argent, a *Lion Saliant* Gules, by the Name of *Felbridg*. Felbridge.

Sable, a *Lion Saliant* Argent, by the Name of *Sturmy*. Sturmy.

Gules, a *Lion Saliant* Argent, by the Name of *Salisbury*. Salisbury.

When the *Lion* prosecutes his Prey, he pursueth the same Leaping, or Saliant, which action he never useth when he is Chased in Fight, but is always Passant.

7. Or, a *Lion Rampant Double Liste* Azure, born by *Simon Mason* of *Great Mas.n.* *Gransden* in *Huntington-shire* Gent.

8. Sable, two *Lion Cells Rampant Combatant* Or, born by *Nicholas Carter* of Carter. *Willesborrow* in *Kent*, and of *London* Dr. in Physick.

Leigh saith, That these two *Lions* were of sundry Regions which strove for Government, for the *Lion* is as desirous of Mastery, as a Courageous Prince is ambitious of Honour.

Azure, two *Lions Rampant Gardant Combatant* Argent, born by Sir *Jacob Gar-* Garrard. *rard* of *Langford* in *Norfolk* Baronet.

I 4

9. Azure,

9. Azure, two *Lioncells Rampant Endorsed* Or.

This Coat is said to be born by *Achilles* at the Siege of *Troy*; and *Leigh* supposeth it to be a Combat intended between two Valiant Men who both met in the Field, but the Prince favouring them taketh the Matter into his hands, and then they turn back to back, and so leave the Field.

10. Or, a *Lion Passant* Gules, by the Name of *Games*.

Games.

Or, a *Lion Passant* Sable, by the Name of *Pynoke*.

Pynoke.

Sable, a *Lion Passant* Or, by the Name of *Taylor*.

Taylor.

Sable, a *Lion Passant* Or, by the Name of *Field*.

Field.

Ermine, a *Lion Passant* Gules, by the Name of *Drew*.

Drew.

Ermine, a *Lion Passant* Sable, by the Name of *Wither*.

Wither.

11. Azure, a *Lion Passant Gardant* Or, born by Sir *John Bromfield* of *Suffolk* place in *Southwark* Knight.

Bromfield.

Azure, a *Lion Passant Gardant* Or, born by *William Thompson* of the middle Temple *London* Esquire.

Thompson.

Argent, a *Lion Passant Gardant* Sable by the Name of *Stone*.   Argent,

Stone.

Argent, a *Lion Passant Gardant* Gules, by the Name of *Querleton.*

Gules, a *Lion Passant Gardant* Or, by the Name of *Brett.*

Gules, a *Lion Passant Gardant* Argent, by the Name of *Redeshall.*

The *Lion Passant* seemeth to go with more Confidence and Resolution, but the *Gardant* with more Vigilancy and Circumspection.

12. Argent, two *Lioncells Counter Passant* Gules, the upermoft towards the Siniſter fide of the *Eſcocheon,* both *Coloured* Or.

13. Gules, a *Lion Sejant* Argent.

Although this Geſture hath affinity with the *Lion Couchant,* yet the difference is eafily to be obferved.

14. Gules, a *Lion* between fix *Croſs Croſslets* Argent, born by Sir *Halſwell Tynte,* of *Halſwell* in the Pariſh of *Goat-hurſt* in *Sommerſet-ſhire* Baronet.

The *Lion* muft not be thought to be compelled to *Couch,* but that he hath fo fettled himfelf of his own accord ; for it is contrary to his Nature, to be compelled to any thing by Chaſtifement, and a generous mind is eafier to be led then drove.

15. Azure,

15. Azure, a *Lion Dormant* Or.

'Tis faid, That the *Lion* fleepeth with his Eyes open, being an Emblem to *Governours*, whofe Vigilancy fhould fhew it felf, when others are moft at reft and fecure.

Some are of Opinion, That the *Lion* fhould not be made *Gardant*, affirming that to be the property of the *Leopard*. The generous Nature of the *Lion*, is difcerned by his plentiful Shaggy Locks which cover his neck and fhoulders, and doth fhew his Noble Courage, efpecially if curled and fhort; alfo the thicknefs of the *Lions Mane*, is a Teftimony of his generous Birth, and by the fame he is diftinguifhed from the Baftard Race of *Leopards*, begotten by the Adulterous *Lionefs* and the *Parde*, which are Naturally deprived of this Noble Mark, nor have they the Courage.

To *Lions*, *Bares*, *Wolves*, and other Beafts of Prey, Nature hath given fharp *Teeth* and *Tallons*, for the feizing and keeping their Prey, and therefore in the *Blazoning* of *Beafts*, their *Teeth* and *Tallons* muft not be omitted, and for expreffing them, fay Armed of fuch and fuch a Colour, which is always Gules or Azure,

and

Lions Rampant

and contrary to the Colour of them.

All *Beasts* of *Prey* in their going do contract their *Tallons* within their Flesh, to keep them sharp for the tearing their Prey, which otherwise would be blunt, and so become useless to them.

Other Examples of

LIONS RAMPANT.

1. S Aphir, a *Lion Rampant* Pearl, born by the Right Honourable *John* Lord Crew, Baron of *Stean* in *Northamp-* *ton shire*, &c.　*Ld. Crew.*

Argent, a *Lion Rampant* Sable, charged on the Shoulder with a *Mullet* Or, born by Sir *Thomas Mompesson* of *Bathampton* in *Wilt-shire*, Knight.　*Mompesson*

Vert, a *Lion Rampant* Or, born by *Ar-* *thur Shaen* of *Great Kewe* in *Surrey*, Esq; Son and Heir of Sir *James Shaen* of the said place, Knight and Baronet.　*Shaen.*

2. Vert, a *Lion Rampant* between three *Trefoyles Slipped* Or, born by *Thomas She-* *ridan*　*Sheridan.*

ridan of *Cavan* in the Province of *Ulster* in *Ireland*, Esquire.

3. Pearl, a *Lion Rampant* Ruby, between three *Pheons* Diamond, born by the Right Honourable *John Egerton*, Earl *Bridgwater*, Viscount *Barkley*, and Baron of *Elesmer*, Lord Lieutenant of *Buckingham-shire*, and one of the Lords of His Majesties most Honourable Privy Council, &c.

Earl of Bridgwater

This Coat is also born by *John Egerton* of *Broxton* in *Cheshire*, Esquire, Eldest Son of Sir *Phillip Egerton* of *Egerton* and *Outon*, in the said County Knight.

Egerton.

4. Argent, a *Lion Rampant* between three *Cross Croslets Fitche* Gules, born by Sir *John Bowyer* of *Kingspersley* in *Stafford-shire*, Knight and Baronet.

Bowyer.

5. Ermine, a *Lion Rampant* Gules, within a *Border* Sable, born by Sir *William Pritchard* of the City of *London* Knight, Lord-*Mayor* thereof *Anno.* 1684.

Pritchard.

6. Gules on a *Pale* Or, a *Lion Rampant* Sable, born by *John Darnall* of the *Middle Temple* London, Esquire.

Darnall.

7. *Barry* of 10 Argent and Azure, over all a *Lion Rampant* Gules, born by *Richard Stratford* of *Hayling* and *Neither-Getting* in *Glocester-shire* Gent. descended from

Stratford.

from the *Stratfords* of *Farmcot* in the said County.

8. Azure, *Flory* a *Lion Rampant* Argent, born by Sir *John Holland* of *Quidenham* in *Norfolk*, Baronet. — *Holland.*

9. Pearl, *Semy de Cinquefoyls* Ruby, a *Lion Rampant* Diamond, born by the Right Honourable *William Pierrepont*, Earl of *Kingston* upon *Hull*, Viscount *Newark* upon *Trent*, Baron of *Holme Pierrepont*, *Manvers*, and *Herris*. — *Earl of Kingston.*

And by *Gervas Pierrpmont* of *Tonge Castle* in *Shropshire*, Esquire. — *Pierrepont.*

Sable, *Semy de Cinquefoils* a *Lion Rampant* Argent, born by Sir *Thomas Clifton* of *Clifton* in *Lancashire*, Baronet. — *Cliffien.*

10. *Per Bend Sinister* Ermine, and Ermines, over all a *Lion Rampant* Or, born by Sir *Roger Mostin* in *Flint-shire*, Baronet. — *Mostin.*

This Coat is also born by Sir *John Trevor* of *Brynkynalt* in *Denby-shire*, Knight: — *Trevor.*

11. *Girony* of 4 or and Azure, a *Lion Rampant* Counterchanged, born by *John Gould* of *Broadnemett* in *Devonshire*, Gentleman. — *Gould.*

12. *Girony* of 8 Pieces Ermine, and Ermines a *Lion Rampant* Or, born by Sir *Trevor Williams* of *Langibby* Castle in *Monmouthshire* Baronet. — *Williams.*

13. Sable

13. Sable a *Lion Rampant* Argent depressed with a *Bendlet* Gules, born by Sir *John Churchill* of *Churchill* in *Sommorsetshire*, Knight.

Churchill.

14. Argent, a *Bend* between two *Lions Rampant* Sable, born by Sir *John Osborn* of *Chicksands* in *Bedfordshire*, Barronet.

Osborn.

15. Ermine three *Lions Rampant* Gules, by the name of *Chudley* in *Devonshire*.

Chudley.

16. Argent, three *Lions* Rampant, and a *cheif* Azure, born by *Samuel Grant* of *Crundal* in *Hantshire*, and of the *Inner Temple* London, Esquire.

Grant.

17. Per *Pale* Saphir and Ruby, three *Lions* Rampant Pearl, born by the Right Honourable the Earl of *Pembrook* and *Montgomery*, Baron *Herbert* of *Shurland*, *Cardiff*, *Ross* of *Kendale*, *Parr*, *Marmion*, and Sir *Quintin*, Lord of the Lordships of *Usk*, *Carleon*, *Newport* and *Treleg*.

Earl of Pembrook.

By the Right Honourable *William Herbert* Earl and Baron of *Powis*, &c.

Earl of Powis.

By the Right Honourable *Edward* Lord *Herbert* Baron of *Cherbury*, and *Castle-Island* in *Ireland*.

Ld Herbert

By the Honourable *Arthur Herbert*, Esquire, Admiral and Commander in Cheif

Herbert.

Cheif of His Majesties Fleet in the *Mediterranean Seas* Anno 1683, and one of the Right Honourable the *Commiſſioners* of the *Admiralty.*

By Sir *Thomas Herbert* of *Trinlern* in *Monmouth-ſhire*, Baronet. *Herbert.*

By Sir *Matthew Herbert* of *Bromfield* in *Shropſhire.*

This Coat is alſo born by Sir *William Jones* of *Slowey* in *Sommerſetſhire*, Knight.

By *Edward Proger* Eſquire, one of the Grooms of His *Majeſties Bedchamber.*

18. Pearl, ſix *Lyons Rampant* Diamond, born by the Right Honourable *Thomas Savage*, Earl *Rivers*, Viſcount *Colcheſter* and *Rock Savage*, Lord *Darcy*, and *Baron* of *Chich*, &c. *Earl Rivers*

19. Ermine, on a *Cheif* Azure, three *Lions Rampant* Or, born by Sir *Anthony Ancher* of *Biſhopsbourn* in *Kent*, Knight and *Baronet.* *Ancher.*

Other

Other Examples of

LIONS PASSANT.

Earl of Northampton.

1. **D**iamond, a *Lion Passant Gardant* Topaz, between three *Helmets* Pearl, born by the Right Honourable *James* Earl of *Northampton*, Baron *Compton* of *Compton*, Lord Leiutenant of *Warwickshire*, *Constable* of the *Tower* of *London*, and one of the Lords of His *Majesties* most Honourable *Privy Councel*, &c.

Wolstonbolom.

2. Azure, a *Lion Passant* between three *Pheons* heads Or, born by Sir *Thomas Wolstonholom* of *Minsingden* in the Parish of *Edmonton* in *Middlesex* Baronet.

Hacket.

Three Sable, three *Piles* Argent on a *Cheif* of the second a *Lion Passant* Gules, born by Sir *Andrew Hacket* of *Moxhull* in *Warwickshire* Knight.

4. Or a *Lion Passant* Sable, in Cheif, three *Piles* of the second, born by Captain

ions. Pasant

tain *John* Logan of *Ibury* in *Oxfordſhire,* Logan.
Eſquire.

5. Argent, on a *Feſs* Gules between two *Lions Paſſant Gardent* Sable, a *Flower de lis* Or, between two *Creſcents* Argent, born by the Honourable Sir *Henry Good-* Goodrick. *rick* of *Ribſton Park* in *Yorkſhire,* Knight and *Baronet* His *Majeſty's Envoy Extraordinary* to the King of *Spain* Anno $168\frac{2}{3}$.

6. Argent, two *Lions Paſſant Gardant* Azure, born by Sir *Thomas Hanmer* Hanmer. of *Hanmer* in *Flitſhire* Baronet, and of Sir *John Hanmer* of the *Middle Temple,* London, Knight.

Or, two *Lions paſſant Gardant* Sable, born by Sir *James Ruſhurſt* of *Milaſt* Ruſhurſt. *Green* in *Eſſex,* Barronet.

Gules, two *Lions Paſſant Gardant* Argent, born by Sir *Nicholas L'eſtrange* of *Hulſton* in *Norfolk* Baronet, and by *Roger L'eſtrange* of Saint *Giles* in the L'eſtrange. *Fields* in *Middleſex,* Eſquire.

7. Gules, two *Bars* Ermine in Cheif a *Lion Paſſant* parted Per Pale Or, and Argent, by the name of *Hill* of *Nor-* Hill. *folk.*

8. *Ermine,* a *Saltier* and *Cheif,* Gules, on the laſt a *Lion Paſſant Gardant* Or, born by *Ivers Armine* of *Oſgodby* in *Lanca-* Armine. *ſhire,*

K

shire, and of *Ketton* in *Rutlandshire*, Esq;

9. Or, three *Lions Paffant* Sable born
Carew.   by Sir *Thomas Carew* of *Hackcomb* in *Devonshire* Barronet.

Sable, three *Lions Paffant* Argent, born
English.   by *Thomas English* of *Buckland* in *Maid-
ston* in *Kent*, Efquire.

10. Argent, three *Lions Paffant Gar-
Brogrve.*   *dant* Gules, born by *Thomas Brograve* of
Hamels in *Hertfordshire*, Barronet.

11. Ruby, three *Lions Paffant Gardant* Per Pale Or and Argent, born by
the Right Honourable *William O' Brion*,
Earl and Baron *Infiquin*, and Baron of
Burren in *Ireland*, and one of the Lords
of His Majefties moft Honourable Privy
Councel for that Kingdom.

12. Azure a *Fefs Wavey*, between
three *Lions Paffant* Or, by the name of
Hawes.   *Hawes.*

From whole Lions *I* fhall *proceed to the
parts thereof.*

folio
147
f Lio

Examples of the

PARTS of LIONS.

1. A Rgent, a *Lions head erazed* Vert.

2. Ruby, a *Cheveron* between three *Lions heads* erazed Pearl, born by the Right Noble *Chriftopher* Duke of *Albemarle*, Earl of *Torrington* Baron *Monk* of *Potheridge*, *Beauchamps* and *Teys*, Knight of the *Garter*, Captain of His Majefties Life *Guard*, Lord Leiutenant of *Effex* and *Devonfhire*, one of the *Gentlemen* of His *Majefties Bedchamber*, and one of the Lords of his moft Honourable *Privy Councel*, &c.

Azure, a *Cheveron* between three *Lions heads* erazed Or, born by Sir *Hugh Windham* of *Silton* in *Dorfetfhire* Knight, one of the *Juftices* of His Majefties *Court* of *Common Pleas* at *Weftminfter*.   And is

K 2   alfo

Windham. alſo born by *Thomas Windham* of *Tale* in *Devonſhire* Eſquire, one of the *Grooms* of His *Majeſties Bedchamber*, third Son of Sir *Edmund Windham* of *Cathanger* in *Sommerſetſhire*, Knight *Marſhal* of His *Majeſties Houſhold.*

3. Or, three *Bars* Azure, on a *Canton Gules*, a *Lions head erazed* Argent, born *Cox.* by *Thomas Cox* M. D. *Phyſitian* in Ordinary to His Majeſty King *Charles* the Second. And is alſo born by *Daniel Cox* of *London* Dr. in Phyſick.

4. Ruby, a *Bezant* between three *Demy Lions Rampant* Pearl, born by the *Earl of* Right Honourable *Henry* Earl of *Arling-* *Arlington.* ton, Viſcount *Thetford*, Knight of the *Garter*, Lord *Chamberlain* of His Majeſties houſhold, and one of the *Lords* of His *Majeſties* Honourable *Privy Councel.* And is born by the Right Honourable Sir *John* *Lord Oſ-* *Bennet* Knight of the *Bath*, and Baron of *weſtre.* *Oſweſtre*, &c.

Bennet. Alſo by *John Bennet* of *Abington* in *Cambridgeſhire*, Eſquire.

5. Azure, two *Bars Wavey* Ermine, on a *Chief* Or, a *Demy Lion* Sable, born *Smith.* by Sir *James Smith* of the City of *London* Knight and *Alderman.*.

6. Or

6. Or, out of the midſt of a *Feſs* Sable, a *Lion Rampant Naiſſant* Gules, by the name of *Emme*. *Emme.*

This Form of Blazon is peculiar to all living things that ſhall be found iſſuing out of the midſt of ſome ordinary, or common charge.

7. *Vert*, three *Quarterfoils* Argent, each charged with a *Lions head Erazed*, Sable, born by *Thomas Plot* Eſquire, Secretary to his Highneſs the great Duke of *Tuſcany*; deſcended of the Family of the *Plots Sparſhott* in *Berkſhire*. *Plot.*

8. Argent, two *Lions Paws* erected in *Saltier*, the dexter ſurmounted of the ſiniſter Azure.

9. Sable, two *Lions Paws* iſſuing out of a dexter and ſiniſter baſe points erect in form of a *Cheveron* Argent, by the name of *Frampton*. *Frampton.*

10. Gules, three *Lions Paws* or *Gambes* Erazed Argent, born by *Richard Newdigate* of *Ardbury* of *Warwickſhire*, Eſquire. *Newdigate.*

11. Azure, three *Lions Paws* couped and erected Argent, by the name of *Uſher*. *Uſher.*

12. Argent, three *Lions Tails* erected and erazed Gules. *Cork.*

K 3

The

The *Lion* hath great ſtrength in his *Tail*, and his much motion thereof is a ſure ſign of Anger. When he intends to aſſail his Enemy he ſtirreth up his courage by often beating his back and ſides with his *Tail*, and when he is hunted the better to eſcape his *Purſuers* (with his *Tail* as he goeth) he ſweepeth out his footſteps and leaveth no tract behind him.

    Theſe and the like *Parts* of *Lions*, and all other *Beaſts* are born on, and between, any of the *Ordinaries*.

    From *Lions* I ſhall proceed to *Elephants*, *Horſes*, and other *Beaſts*.

Examples of Other

BEASTS *in whole and in part.*

1. **G**Ules, an *Elephant* paſſant Argent, tusked Or, by the name of *Elpington*.

Elpington.

    The *Elephant* is a Beaſt of great ſtrength but of greater wit and docility ſurpaſſing

furpaffing all other *Beafts*, and is fo ambitious that if they are praifed they
will kill themfelves with labour, his
ftrength appears in that he carrieth on his
back in a *Caftle of Wood* about thirty
men, as is accuftomary in the *Eaftern
Countries* to make ufe of them in their
Wars.

2. Or a *Fefs* Gules between three E-
lephants heads erazed Sable, born by *John Fountain.
Fountain* of *Melton* on the Hill in *York-
fhire*, Efquire.

3. Purpure, a *Probofcide Trunk* or
Snout of en *Elephant* in *Pale* couped, flexed and reflexed in form of an S Or.

The *Elephant* hath great ftrength inthis
part and ufeth it for his hand, as well
to feed himfelf, as for all ufes of Agility.

4. Or, an *Affes* head erazed Sable, by
the name of *Hackwell.* Hackwell.

The *Afs* is the lively Embleme of
patience : From this *Beaft*, and the
Horfe cometh the *Mule* which being fo
produced doth not bring forth young as
other *Beafts.*

5. Pearl, three *Bulls Paffant* Diamond,
This was the Coat of the Right Honoura-
ble *Anthony* Earl of *Shaftsbury*, Baron Earl of
Aftley of *Wimborn* Saint *Giles*, Lord fhaftsbury.

K 4   Cooper

Cooper of *Pawlet*, &c.

The *Bull* is the Ringleader amongst ruther *Beasts*, and through hope of his encrease of breed he is priviledged to rang freely in all Pastures.

The *Bull* being *Gelt* changeth not only his nature but his name to an *Ox*. And it is said that the *Athenians* to express their gratefulness for the laborious travel of the *Ox*, did stamp it's Figure on a certain *Coyn* called a *Didrachma*.

6. Sable, a *Cheveron* Ermine between three *Bulls head cabosed* Argent, born by *Thomas Sanders* of little *Ireton* in *Derby-shire*, Esquire.

Sanders.

7. Pearl, three *Bulls head erazed* Diamond, born by the Right Honourable Sir *John Skeffington* of *Fisherwick* in *Stafford-shire*, Barronet, Baron of *Loughneugh*, Viscount *Massereen*, *Custos Rotolorum*, and Governour of the County of *London-derry* and Town of *Coleraine* and one of the *Lords* of His *Majesty* most Honourable *Privy Councel* for *Ireland*

Lord Mas-sereue.

8. Gules, a *Goat Passant* Argent, by the name of *Baker*.

Baker.

The *Goat* is not so hardy as politick.

9. Gules, a *Stag standing* at *Gaze* Argent

gent, attired Or, by the name of
Jones.

Jones.

The *Stag* is a goodly Beaft, full of
State in his *Gate* and *View*, and amongft
Beafts of *Chafe* is efteemed the cheif
for *Game.* It is obferved that when he
findeth himfelf Fat he lodgeth in obfcure
places to avoid Chafing. This Beaft is
indued with two excellent faculties above
others to wit quicknefs of hearing, and
fwiftnefs of Foot, which makes the Chafe
more long and difficult.

10. Argent, a *Stag* fpringing forward
Gules.

Pliny faith that the Horns of this Beaft
whilft they are growing are fo mollified
with Wax that they may be made capable
of divers *Impreffions.* All *Horns* are hal‹
low except towards the tip, but the *Deers*
are folid throughout.

11. *Vert*, on a *Cheveron* between three
Bucks triping Or, as many *Trefoils flipped*
Gules, born by Sir *Lumbley Robinfon* of
Kentwell-hall in *Suffolk* Barronet, Son and
Heir of Sir *Thomas Robinfon*, chief *Pro-
thonotary* of his *Majefties Court* of *Common
Pleas*, deceafed.

Robinfon.

The *Buck* is a worthy *Beaft*, and hath
much of the properties of the *Stag*,
but

but cometh short of his statelinefs and boldnefs.

12. Or, three *Bucks head couped* proper, born by Sir *Peter Colleton* of Saint *James's Fields* in *Middlesex*, Baronet.

Colleton.

The Bearing of the *Head* of any living thing betokeneth jurifdiction and Authority to adminifter Juftice, and to execute *Laws*.

13. *Saphir*, a *Stags* head Pearl, born by the Right Honourable *George Leg*, Baron of *Dartmouth*, Mafter General of the *Ordnance*, Leiutenant of *Alcebolt*, and *Wolmer* Foreft in *Hantfhire*, Mafter of the Horfe to his Royal Highnefs *James* Duke of *York*, Admiral of His *Majefties Fleet* of Ships in the *Mediterranean*, *Anno* 1683, and one of the *Lords* of His *Majefties* moft Honourable *Privy Counfel*, &c.

Lord Dartmouth.

14. *Saphir*, a *Bucks head cabofed* Topaz, vulned in the forehead proper, born by the Right Honourable *Kenneth*, M' *Renzie*, Earl of *Seafort*, Lord M' *Kenzie* and *Kentail*, Baron of *Ardelu*, *Iflandonan* and *Lews*, Sheriff principal of the Shires of *Rofs*, and North *Nafs*, &c.

Earl of Seafort.

15. Diamond, three *Bucks heads cabofed* Pearl, *attired* Topaz, born by the Right

folio

Beasts in whole,
and in part.

Right Honourable *William* Earl of De-
vonshire, Baron *Cavendish* of *Hardwick*
Lord Leiutenant of *Derby-shire*, &c.

  16. Azure, a *Fess* between three *Ti-
gers heads erazed* Or, born by Sir *Henry
Hunlock* of *Wingerworth* in *Derbyshire*,
Baronet.

  17. Argent, a *Cheveron* between three
Attires of a *Stag* fixed to the *Scalp* Sable, by the Name of *Cockes*.

  18. Or, three *Attires* of a *Stag* born
paly *Barry* Sable.

Earl of
Devonshire

Hunlock

Cockes.

Other Examples of

BEASTS *in whole and in part.*

  1. Sable, a *Fess* between three *Horses
passant* Argent, born by Sir *Thomas
Stamp* of *London*, Knight and Alderman.

Stamp.

  A *Horse* erected, (that is bolt upright)
may be termed enraged, but his noblest
Action

Action is exprest in a faliant form. The *Horse* of all *Beasts* for mans use is esteemed the most noble, and useful either in Peace or War, he is naturally stubborn, fierce and pround, and of all *Beasts* there is none that vaunteth more after Victory obtained, or dejected if vanquished, and none more prone to *Battle*, or desirous of revenge.

2. Gules, a *Horses head* couped Argent, this was the Coat of Sir *Thomas Marsh* of *Darkes* in the Parish of *South Mimums* in *Middlesex*, Knight deceased.

Marsh.

3. Argent, a *Unicorn seiant* Sable, horned Or, by the name of *Harling*.

Harling.

The *Unicorn* takes his name from his one Horn which grows on his Forehead, yet there is another Beast called a *Rinoceros* which hath but one Horn, but that doth grow on his Snout.

The *Unicorn* is no less worthy of remark for his Vertue then for his Strength in that his *Horn* is said to be a powerful *Antidote* against poyson, in so much as (according to the general opinion) the wild Beast (for fear of the venemous *Serpents*) use not to drink before he hath stirred the *Waters* with his *Horn*; he is

said

said to be of such a great and haughty mind that he will never be taken alive, but rather will be killed; being by nature of so untamely a disposition.

4. Gules, an *Unicorn* triping Argent, armed Or, by the name of *Muster-ton*.   *Musterton.*

5. Vert, three *Unicorns* in *Pale currant* Argent, armed Or, by the name of *Farington.*   *Farington.*

6. Sable, a *Camel passant* Argent.

This *Beast* doth surpass the *Horse*, not only for strength (his common burthen being 1000 *l.* weight,) but for his swiftness in Travel.

7. Argent, a *Bore passant* Gules, armed Or, by the name of *Trewarthen.*   *Trewarthen*

The *Bore* though he wanteth *Horns* is no way defective in his Weapon of defence or rather of offence, to wit his strong and sharp *Tusks*, being reckoned for the most absolute *Champion* amongst the *Wild Beasts*. In his fight he is so cruel, and stomackful that he foameth all the while for rage, and against the time of any encounter he *often* whetteth his *Tusks* to make them more peircing, and he beareth the encounter with a noble courage.

8. To-

8. Topaz, three *Bores heads* erazed and erected Diamond armed of the firſt, born by the Right Honourable *George* Lord *Booth* Baron *de la Mere* of *Dunham Maſſey* in *Cheſhire.*

Lord *De la Mere.*

And by Sir *Robert Booth* of *Salford* in *Lancaſhire,* Knight, Lord *Cheif Juſtice* of his Majeſties *Court of Common Pleas* in *Ireland,* and one of his Majeſties moſt Honourable *Privy Councel* for the ſaid Kingdom.

Baoth.

And is alſo born by *Richard Booth* of the City of *London,* Eſquire.

9. Argent, a *Cheveron* between three *Bores head* erazed Sable, born by *Theophilus Oglethorp* of the Pariſh of Saint *Martins* in the *Fields* in *Middleſex Leiutenant Collonel* to his Royal *Highneſs*'s Troop of his *Majeſties* Horſe *Guards,* &c.

Oglethorp.

10. Azure, three *Cups* Or, out of each a *Bores head* erected Argent, born by Sir *John Bolles* of *Scampton* in *Lincolnſhire,* Baronet.

Bolles.

11. Azure, a *Toiſon d*' Or within a *Treaſure* of *Scotland* Or, born by Sir *Robert Jaſon* of Broad *Somerford* in *Wiltſhire,* Baronet.

Jaſon.

12. Argent, a *Cheveron* Sable, between three *Rams heads* erazed Azure, born by
Sir

Sir *John Bendish* of *Steple-Bumsted* in *Essex* Bendish.
Baronet.

The *Ram* is a Captain of the whole flock, and his ſtrength conſiſteth in his head.

Other Examples of

BEASTS.

1. ARgent, a *Tiger paſſant regardant,* gazing in a looking Glaſs all proper.

The *Tiger* is ſaid to be a *Beaſt* of great cruelty and exceeding ſwift of Foot, whence ſome think the River *Tigris* took its name.

It is reported that when thoſe that go to rob her of her young, do uſe a policy to detain their Dam from following them, by caſting ſundry *Looking Glaſſes* in the way, on which ſhe uſeth to gaze long upon whether it be to behold her
own

own beauty, or becauſe when ſhe ſeeth her ſhape in the Glaſs ſhe thinketh ſhe ſeeth one of her young ones; but by this means they eſcape her.

2. Argent, a *Bear Rampant* Sable, muſled Or, by the name of *Barnard*.   *Barnard.*

The *Bear* by nature is a cruel *Beaſt*, and in its combates uſeth no leſs policy then ſtrength. The *Female* is moſt cruelly enraged againſt any that hurts her young, or robbeth her of them.

3. Argent, three *Bears heads erazed* Sable, *Muſled* Or, born by Sir *James Langham* of *Cottes-brook* in *Northamptonſhire*, Knight and Baronet.   *Langham.*

By Sir *William Langham* of *Walgrave* in the ſaid County Knight. And by Sir *Stephen Langham* of *London* Knight, Sons of Sir *John Langham*, Baronet deceaſed.

4 Gules, a *Wolf preyent* Argent, born by Sir *Edward Low* of *New Sarum*, in *Wiltſhire* Kt. one of the *Maſters* of the high Court of *Chancery*.   *Low.*

The *Wolf* by nature is a greedy, ravenous and cruel Creature, and a great Enemy to the poor harmleſs *Sheep*; inſomuch that (for the publick good) Laws have been made to give a gratuity to

thoſe

those that kill, or take any of them alive.

Macidon Grand-child of *Cham* the Son of *Noah* bore a *Wolf* when he went under the Conduct of *Osius*. And the Image of a *Wolf* was set up at *D. . . .* before *Apollo* who was called *Lycoctones* a *Wolf* killer and he was rewarded by the Laws of *Draco* and *Solon* that killed or took alive this Creature.

5. Argent, on a *Bend* Vert, three *Wolves heads* erazed of the Field, born by Sir *Richard Middelton* of *Chirk Castle* in *Denbighshire* Baronet. *Myddelton.*

And by Sir *Thomas Middleton* of *Stansted Mount-Fitchet* in *Essex* Knight.

6. Vert, a *Greyhound currant* Argent, collored Gules, studded Or, born by *Richard Blome* of *Abergwlly* in *Caermardenshire*, Esquire, by *John Blome* of *Sevenoke* in *Kent*, Gentleman, and by *Richard Blome* of *London* Gentleman, the Author of this Tract of *Heraldry*. *Blome.*

The *Dog* whether it be for Pleasure and Game in the Field, as the Greyhound, and the *Hound* (of which there are several forts as the *Buck hound*, *Bloodhound*, *Harier*, *Grey-hound* and the like; or for safe-guard at home as the *Mastiff*

  deserv-

deſerveth a very high eſtimation, and of all *Dogs* thoſe of Chaſe are the moſt deſerving in *Heraldry*.

It is obſerved that there is ſcarce any vertue incident to a Man, but there are ſome reſemblances thereof in the ſundry kinds of *Dogs*; and the *Maſtiff* hath that undaunted courage and true love to his Maſter that he will take his part even to death, inſomuch that the *Romans* took *Maſtiffs* hence to carry in their Army inſtead of *Souldiers*; others there are that when they happen to be loſt will refuſe meat to eat untill they ſee their Maſters again; others are to be admired for their excellent properties in looking to their *Maſters* Goods, others in fetching, carrying, and finding out any loſt thing that they are enjoyned to do; and others in purſuing any thing or Game in the Chaſe by the ſcent of its foot.

7. Argent, three *Grey-hounds* in *Pale currant* Sable collered Or, born by Sir *Cleve More* of *More-hall*, and *Bank-hall* in *Lancaſhire* Baronet, and by Sir *John More* of *London*, Knight and Alderman, late Lord Mayor thereof.

Gules, three *Grey-hounds currant* in Pale Argent, collered of the Field, born by by Sir *Thomas Mauleverer* of *Allerton-Mauleverer* in *Yorkshire*, Baronet.

8. *Argent*, two *Bars* Sable charged with three *Trefoils* of the Field, in *Chief* a *Greyhound* currant of the second, born by *William Palmer* of *Ladgrave* in *Warwickshire*, Esquire.

9. *Gules*, a *Talbot passant* Or, a Chief Ermine, born by *Thomas Chaffin* of *Chettle* in *Dorsetshire* Esquire.

10. *Argent*, two *Reynards* or *Foxes counter-Saliant* in *Bend*, the dexter surmounted of the finister Saltire wise Gules by the name of *Kadrod-Hard* of *Wales*.

The *Fox* for his great wit and fubtilty doth furpafs all Beafts, and is compared to the crafty *Lawyer*.

11. Ermine, on a *Fefs* Gules, a *Fox passant* Or, born by Sir *Thomas Proby* of *Elton-hall* in *Huntingtonshire*, Knight. And by *John Proby* of the middle *Temple London*, Esquire.

12. Or, three *Foxes heads* erazed Gules, a *Border* Argent charged with eight *Flower de lis* Azure, born by *Nevinson Fox* of *Stadbrook* in *Suffolk* Esquire.

13. Gules, an *Ermine* proper.

The *Skin* of this little Beaft is an exceeding rich Fur ufed for the Lining of

L 2

Kings

Kings and *Princes* Robes, and is that Fur so much used in *Heraldry* called *Ermine.*

14. Argent, three *Cat a mountains passant* in *Pale* Sable, born by Sir *Jonathan Keat* of *Pauls Walden* in *Hertford-shire*, Baronet.

There is no Creature that contendeth so much for liberty as the *Cat*, and therefore the *Dutch* formerly bore it for their Ensign.

It is also a Creature of such great use that no house can well be without one for the destroying Vermine.

15. Argent, two *Squirrels Sciant endorsed* Gules, born by Sir *Thomas Samwel* of *Upton* and *Gayton* in the County of *Northamptonshire* Baronet.

This little *Creature* is much to be commended for his great industry in gathering, and providing his food in the Summer for the Winter, which should be an example to the slothful man who regardeth nothing but from hand to mouth.

16. Argent, three *Coneys* Sable, by the name of *Stroud.*

From the *Coney* 'tis said that men first learnt the Art of undermining and sub-

verting

Animalls.

verting of *Cities*, *Castles*, and *Towers*, by the Industry of *Pioneers*.

    From *Beasts* I shall proceed to *Animals*.

Examples of

ANIMALS.

1. VERT, a *Tortois passant*, Argent, born by Sir *Charles Gawdy* of *Crows-hill* in *Debenham* in *Suffolk*, Kt. and Baronet. By *Charles Gawdy* of *Stapeston*, and by *Anthony Gawdy* of *Ipswich* both of the said County Esquires.

Gawdy.

Tortoises, live both by Land and Sea, and are much esteemed as well for their Vertues, and operation, as for the delicacy of their Shells used for divers curious works, and their flesh to eat. They are Enemies to *Vipers* destroying both *Snails* and *Worms* that eat the *Fruits*. The Shells of the *Arcadian Tortoises* are very

great of which they make *Harps* whereof *Mercury* is said to be the first inven-
tor, who finding a *Tortoise* upon the *Rocks*
after the falling of the River *Nilus*, the
flesh being consumed, and the sinews
dried up, he stroke them with his hand,
and making a kind of musical sound he
framed it into a *Harp*.

2. Azure, a *Tortoise erected* Or, by the
name of *Cooper*.

Cooper.

3. Argent, a *Cheveron* between three
Mouls, or *Wants* Sable, born by *Richard*.
Twisleton of *Drax* in the *West riding* of
Yorkshire Esquire.

Twislleton.

This *Animal* is very pernitious in *Gar-
dens, Orchards*, and other grounds casting
up the Earth in great hillocks with their
Snouts. They are very quick of hearing, and have a good smell.

4. Argent, three *Toads* erected Sable,
by the name of *Betereux*.

Betereux.

Toads and *Frogs* when they sit, hold up
their heads without motion, which stately action *Spencer* in his *Shepheards* Calen-
der calleth the *Lording* of *Frogs*.

5. Or, a *Cobweb* in the *Center* thereof
a *Spider* proper.

The *Spider* may be said to be born
free of the *Weavers* Company, for she
                                        stu-

ftudieth not his *Art*, nor hath his ftuff having her thread out of her womb, from whence fhe laborioufly draweth it, and through the Agility of her Feet fhe weaveth gins and dilateth, contracteth and knitteth them in form of a *Net*, and with the *threads* that fhe draweth out of her body fhe repaireth the fame, and thefe *Webs* are framed with much artificial cunning, and yet are fit for no ufe, but to entangle Flies; and as it is obferved, the Execution of the Law is compared to *Cobwebs*.

Laws like Spiders webs are wrought.
Great Flies efcape, and fmall are caught.

The *Spider* is poifonous, yet her *Web*, although it be drawn out of her *Womb*, is faid to be an *Antidote* againft it.

6. Argent, 11 *Emets* 3, 2, 3, 2, 1, Sable.

By the *Emet*, or *Pifmire*, as indeed by the *Spider* may be fignified a man of great labour, wifdom, and providence in his Affairs: And to thefe little Creatures the flothful man is fent to learn wifdom.

7. Vert, a *Grafs-hopper* in *Fefs paffant* Or,

L 4

In

In the Summer Season the Male *Grass-hoppers* do sing, but the Females are silent.

Amongst the *Athenians Grass-hoppers* were holden for a special note of *Nobility*, and therefore did use to wear in their Hair golden *Grass hoppers*. *Solomon* reckoneth the *Grass hopper* for one of the four small things in the Earth that are full of wisdom, but according to the Fable the *Emet* thinks him otherwise.

8. Gules, an *Adder* nowed Or, by the name of *Nathiley*.

Nathiley.

The *Serpent* is very subtile and prudent, as well to hurt others, as to save himself; and knowing, that his most principal and most weakest part to be his head, he hath the greatest care thereof; this here enfolded may seem as *Guillim* noteth to be one of the Locks of that Monstruous Dame *Medusa*, every Hair of whose Head was said to be a *Snake*, and indeed *Albertus* saith that the Hair of Women taken at some Seasons and laid in Dung will become venemous *Serpents*, which some have supposed to befal that Sex for the ancient familiarity it had at first with that accursed Serpent.

9 Azure

9. Azure, a *Cheveron* between three *Urchins*, or *Hegdhogs* Argent, born by *William Mainston* of *London* Gentleman, lineally defcended from *Thomas Mainston* of *Urchinfield* in *Herefordshire* Gentleman, who lived *Temps Edward* the Third.

The *Hedghogs* may be compared to a *Man* expert in gathering of fubftance, and as it were one that maketh Hay whilft the Sun fhineth.

10. Sable, a *Fefs* between three *Houfe Snails Argent*, by the name of *Shelley*.

The *Snail* though a flow goer yet in time by the conftancy of her Courfe afcendeth to the top of the higheft Tower.

It is Fabled that when the *Hare* was to go a Journey for a Wager with the *Snail*, the *Hare* too confident of his Foot manfhip refolved to take a Nap by the way but the *Snail* well knowing that he had nothing to truft unto but his indefatigable perfeverance came to his Journeys end before the *Hare* awaked.

11. Argent, a *Cheveron* Gules between three *Scorpions* reverfed Sable, by the name of *Cole*.

Scorpions are venemous yet the Oyl

made

made of them is an approved *Antidote* against their own stinging.

Thus much of Animals under which head may be comprehended all those of four or more Feet that lay *Eggs*, as *Crocodiles, Salamanders, Cameleons, Ewtes, Lizards,* &c.

CHAP.

CHAP. IV.

Treats of Fowls *and* Birds *of all sorts, which may be termed* Areal Animals, *and may be considered by their Feet, which are either whole, which resembleth the* Palm *of a* Hand, *and such are the* Swan, Goose, Duck, *and for the most part all* River Fowls : *or divided as the* Eagle, Falcon, Raven, *and the like, and* Birds *of the* Air *as shall appear by the following Examples.*

ALL *Fowls* of what kind soever must be bore in their natural Actions, of *Going, Setting, Standing,* or *Flying.* Concerning the *Beaks* or *Bills,* and Feet of *Birds* all those that either are

whole

whole Footed , or have their Feet divided, and yet have no *Tallons* should be
termed *Membred*; but the *Cock* and all
Birds of *Prey* should be termed Armed ;
and the *Arming*, or Membring them is
always to be of a different Colour from
the Fowl or Bird it self.

It is generally observed that the Females amongst Birds of Prey are the noblest and most hardy which nature hath so
ordered, as being her part to take care,
and to provide for her young.

In the *Blazoning of Fowls* much used
to fly, if their Wings be not displayed
they must be termed close.

The Parts and Members of *Fowls* are
usually born in *Coat Armour* both couped
and erazed, and that on, or between, any
of the *Honourable Ordinaries.*

Birds are of a more noble bearing than
Fish for that they perticipate more of the
Fire and *Air* the noblest Elements.

Examples

Fowle & Birds.

Examples of

FOWL and BIRDS.

1. **G**Ules, a *Swan* Argent, by the name of *Leigham*.

Leigham.

All River *Fowls* have their Tails shorter then *other Birds*, for the length of the Tail doth hinder their *Swiming, Diving,* or *Running.*

The *Swan* is a *Bird* of great Beauty and Strength, and it is said that he useth not his Strength to Prey, or Tyranize over any other *Fowl*, but only to be revenged on such, as first offer him wrong, in which case he often subdueth the *Eagle*, and it is observed that he never encounters with any other of his own kind, but in two cases, the one if any be a Rival in his Love, or offer to *Court* his Mate, he will be revenged to death ; the next is if another do incroach upon his possessi-

on,

on, or place of haunt, he is never quiet until he hath expulsed him.

2. Azure, a *Bend Engrailed* Argent, between two *Signets Royal* proper, born by Sir *Charles Pitfield* of *Hoxton* in the Parish of Saint *Leonards Shoreditch* in *Middlesex* Knight, deceased.

Pitfield.

Azure, three *Swans* Argent, by the name of *Charlton.*

Charlton.

Gules, three *Swans* Argent, by the name of *Bawdrip.*

Bawdrip.

Sable, a *Swan* with her Wings *expanded* Argent, *Membred* Or, within a *Border Engrailed* of the Second, by the name of *More.*

More.

Azure, two *Swans* Argent, between as many *Flanches* Ermine, born by *Samuel Mellish* of the Inner *Temple, London,* Esquire.

Mellish.

3. Sable, a *Cheveron* between three *wild Ducks* Volant proper.

The *Wild Duck* hath many enemies, as *Men, Dogs,* and *Hawks,* yet by their shifts in *Flying, Swimming,* and *Diving,* they often beguile the hope of their pursuers.

4. Argent, a *Stork* Sable, Membred Gules, by the name of *Starkey.*

Starkey.

The *Stork* is a *Bird* most careful of her young,

young, and therefore nature requiteth her care; for their young do take the like care of them in their old Age, whence it is that the *Stork* is the Emblem of a grateful Man, and a dutiful Son. *Ælian* writes of a *Stork*, which bred in the House of one that had a beautiful Wife, which in her Husbands absence used to commit Adultery with one of her meaner Servants, which the *Stork* observing, in gratitude to him who freely gave him *House-room* he flying in the Villains face struck out both his Eyes.

5. Ermine, a *Spread Eagle*, or *Eagle* displayed Gules, born by Sir *Henry Bedingfield* of *Oxborough*, and *Beck hall* in *Norfolk* Baronet. *Bedingfield*

The *Eagle* hath a sharp and *peircing* sight, and soareth so high that oft times she transcendeth the sight of a man. She hath a tender care of her young, and when they are ready to flie taketh them on her Wings, and so soareth with them through the Air to teach them to fly.

6. Argent, a *Spread Eagle* with two *Heads* Sable, born by Sir *John Glynn* of *Glyn. Burcester* alias *Bisister* in *Oxfordshire* Baronet.

7. Gules,

7. Gules, a *Bend* between two *Eagles* displayed Or, born by *Thomas Travel* of Saint *Martins in the Fields* in *Middlesex*, Esquire.

Travel.

8. Vert, three *Eagles* displayed in *Fess* Or, by the name of *Wynn*.

Wynn.

Other Examples of
Eagles.

Azure an *Eagle* displayed *Argent*, born by Sir *Robert Cotton de Bruce* of *Hatley*, Saint *George* in *Cambridgeshire* Knight.

Cotton.

Gules, an *Eagle* displayed Or, born by *Edward Goddard* of *Standen*, by *Thomas Goddard* of *Swindon*, *Richard Goddard* of *Catford*, and by *Edward Goddard* of *Ogbourn* all of *Wiltshire* Esquires.

Goddard.

Argent, an *Eagle* displayed Sable, by the name of *Millington*.

Millington.

Sable, an *Eagle* displayed *Argent*, armed Gules, by the name of *Boyland*.

Boyland.

Argent, an *Eagle* displayed Vert, by the name of *Bilney*.

Bilney.

armed

Or, an *Eagle* displayed Sable, by the name of *Kirkhill*. Kirkhill.

Gules, an *Eagle* displayed Ermine, by the name of *Waxey*. Waxey.

Parted per *Pale* Or, an Argent, an *Eagle* displayed Gules, by the name of *Thomp*-Thompson. son.

Parted per *Pale* Gules and Ermine, an *Eagle displayed* Or, by the name of *Bor*-Bordam. dam.

Parted per *Bend*, Gules and Vert an *Eagle displayed* Or, by the name of *Grave*. Grave.

Azure, three *Eaglets* displayed Or, by the name of *Billesworth*. Billesworth

Or, three *Eaglets displayed* Gules, by the name of *Eglesford*. Eglesford.

Argent, three *Eaglets* displayed Gules by the name of *Eaglesfield*. Eaglesfield

Sable, six *Eaglets displayed* Argent, by the name of *Barantine*. Barantine.

9. Sable, a *Goshawk* Argent, *Perching* upon a *Stock*, fixed in the *Base point* of the *Escocheon* of the second, *Armed, Jes-sed*, and *Billed* Or, by the name of *Weele*. Weele.

Next to the *Eagle* which is reckoned the Sovereign Queen of all *Fowls*, the the *Goshawk*, the *Ger-Falcon*, the *Falcon*,

M and

and other Birds of Prey are the Cheif.

Gules, three *Falcons* Argent, Armed, Jessed and Belled Or, by the name of *Atherton*.

Atherton.

Azure, three *Falcons* Argent, *Armed, Jessed,* and *Belled* Or, by the name of *Pennington*.

Pennington.

Sable, a *Falcon* Argent, Armed Or, by the name of *Yedling*.

Yedling.

10. Gules, a *Cheveron* between three *Facons* Argent, born by *George Hadley* of East *Barnet* in *Hertfordshire* Esquire.

Hadley.

11. Azure, three *Bustards* rising Or, by the name of *Nevill*.

Nevill.

It is observable that all long Shank'd Fowl in their flight do stretch forth their Legs at length to their *Tails*, but the short do truss their Feet up to the midst of their *Bodies*.

12. Or, a *Raven* proper born by Sir *John Corbet* of *Stoke* upon *Teane*, and *Adderley* in *Shropshire* Baronet.

Corbet.

The *Raven* is said to give no food to it's young until she seeth what colour they will be of, and when she seeth them black like her self she is very careful of them.　This Bird is said to live about 100 years, and doth take it's name from it's rapine quality.

13. Gules,

13. Gules, a *Pelican* in her *Neſt*, with *Wings diſplayed*, feeding her young ones Or, vulned proper, by the name of *Carne*.

The *Egyptian Prieſts* as *Farneſius* noteth uſed the *Pelican* for a *Hierogliphick* to ex‑preſs the duties of a Father to his Children.

14. Gules, three *Cocks* Argent, arm‑ed, creſted, and Jolloped Or, by the name of *Cock*.

The *Cock* may not improperly be term‑ed the Knight amongſt *Birds*, being of a noble courage, and alſo prepared to Bat‑tel, having his *Comb* for an *Helmet*, his ſharp and hooked B.ll for a *Faulcheon*, or *Courtlax*, and as a compleat Soldier arm‑ed *a Cap-a-pee*, he hath his Legs armed with *Spurs*. When he is Victor he crow‑eth which gives teſtimony of his Con‑queſt, and when he is vanquiſhed he ſhun‑eth the light, or ſociety of men.

15. Or, three *Swallows*, their Wings cloſe proper, by the name of *Watton*.

The *Swallow* is the welcome harbinger, ſhewing the approach of the Spring.

16. Argent, a *Croſs* Gules between four *Peacocks* Azure, born by the Right Honourable *Francis* Lord *Carington*, Ba‑ron

M 2

Carne.

Cock.

VVatton.

Lord Ca‑*rington.*

ron of *Wotton* in *Warwickshire*, and Viscount *Barreford* in *Ireland*.

The *Peacock* is so proud that when he
erecteth his Fan of Plumes he admireth
himself, and doth display them against
the rayes of the Sun that they may glister
with the greater Glory.

Other Examples of Fowls.

Argent, three *Swans disclosed* Sable,
Folgnardy. by the name of *Folgnaraly.*

Sable, a *Heron* Argent, by the name
Heron.　of *Heron.*

Argent, a *Cock* Gules, Armed, Crested,
Broncham. and Jolloped Or, by the name of *Broncham.*

Argent, a *Raven proper,* by the name of
Morton.　*Morton.*

Sable, a *Falcon* Argent, Armed Or, by
Yedling.　the name of *Yedling.*

Azure, three *Falcons* their *Wings* ex-
Nevile.　panfed Argent, by the name of *Nevile.*

Argent, a *Pelican* in her *Nest,* vulned,
Cantrell. and disclosed Sable, by the name of *Cantrell.*

Azure, three *Pelicans* Or, vulned proper,

Birds

per born by Sir *John Pelham* of *Langton*   *Pelham.*
in *Suſſex* Baronet.

Argent, a *Cock* Gules, Armed, Creſted, and Jolloped Or, by the name of
Brougham.   *Brougham.*

Argent, three *Cocks* Gules, by the name
of *Coliborn.*   *Coliborn.*

Argent, three *Cocks* Sable, Armed,
Creſted, and Jolloped Or, by the name
of *Pomfret.*   *Pomfret.*

Sable, three *Heath Cocks* Argent,
Membred Gules, by the name of *Hathe.*   *Hathe.*

Argent, ſix *More Cocks* Sable, Membred Gules, by the name of *Fitz-*   *Fitz-*
Mores.   *Mores.*

Other Examples of

BIRDS.

1. **P**EARL, on a *Bend* Diamond,
three *Owls* of the Field, born by the
moſt Honourable *George Savill*, Marqueſs
Earl and Viſcount *Hallifax*, and Baron of

 Elaid

Eland in *Yorkshire,* Lord *Privy Seal,* and one of the Lords of his *Majesties* most Honourable Privy Councel, *&c.*

The *Owl* was *Minerva's Bird,* and was born by the *Athenians* for their Armorial Ensign. In *Armoury* he signifies *Prudence, Vigilancy,* and *Watchfulness* by Night.

2. Sable, an *Orle* of *Owls* within an *Escocheon* Argent, born by Sir *Henry* Calverley. *Calverley* of *Eryholme* in *Yorkshire* Knight.

3. Diamond, *Gutte de leau,* on a *Fess* Pearl, three *Cornish Choughs* proper, born LordCorn-by the Right Honourable *Charles* Lord wallis. *Cornwallis,* Baron of *Eye* in *Suffolk,* &c.

4. Argent, a *Cross Potance* between four *Martlets* Sab e, a *Canton* Ermenois, Stringer. born by *Thomas Stringer* of *Bexwells* in *Essex* Esquire.

5. Or an *Escocheon* within an *Orle* of eight *Martlets* Sable, born by Sir *John* Brownlow. *Brownlow* of *Belton* near *Grantham* in *Lincolnshire* Baronet.

The *Martlet* hath *Legs* so short that they can't go, and if they happen to fall upon the ground they can't raise themselves upon their Feet as other *Birds* do to prepare themselves for flight, and for this reason they make their Nests upon *Rocks,* and high places, from whence they may easily take their flight.   6. Per

6. *Per Fess* Gules and Argent, six *Martlets* counterchanged, born by Sir *Jo. Fenwick* of *Wallington* in *Northumberland* Baronet, *Cornet* to the *Queens* Troop of his *Majesties* Guards.   *Fenwick.*

7. Azure, a *Cheveron* between three *Martlets* Argent, born by *Tolemach Duke* of *Lincolns* Inn in *Middlesex* Esquire, *Exigenter* for *London* in the Court of *Common Pleas.*   *Duke.*

8. Gules, a *Cheveron embattuled* Ermine, between three *Martlets* Or, born by the *Honourable* Sir *Francis Withins* of *Eltham* in *Kent* Knight, one of the Justices of his Majesties Court of *Kings Bench Westminster.*   *Withins.*

9. Gules, a *Ferdemolin* Argent, between two *Martlets* Or, born by Sir *William Beversham* of *Millbeck-hall* in *Suffolk* Knight, one of the *Masters* in *Chancery.*   *Beversham.*

10. Sable, on a *Cheveron* between ten *Martlets* Argent, five Plates, or Ogresses born by *Thomas Bard* of *Caversfield* in *Buckinghamshire* Esquire.   *Bard.*

11. Azure, three *Bees volant en arriere* Argent, by the name of *Bye.* The *Bee* is a very profitable *Insect* for its *Wax* and *Honey* which is esteemed a great preser-   *Bye.*

M 4

ver

ver of Nature.   To speak of the properties of the *Bee*, and their Government would be too tedious for this place.

12. Argent, three *Eagles heads* erazed
Sable, by the names of *Yellen*.

Yellen.

13. Argent six *Ostriches feathers* 3, 2,
and 1 Sable, by the name of *Jervis*.

Jervis.

14 Gules, two *Wings impailed* conjoyned in *Fess*, or two *Wings* in *Lure* Or,
by the name of *Seymour*.

Seymour.

15. Sable, an *Eagles Leg* in *Pale erazed
a laquise* Argent, the *Tallons* Gules, by the
name of *Cunhanser*.

Cunhanser.

16. Or, two *Eagles Legs barways* erazed *a la quise* Sable, armed Gules.

Other Examples of Birds.

Herwart.   Argent, an *Owle* Gules, by the name of
Herwart.

Argent, a *Cornish Chough* proper, by the
name of *Trenethyn*.

Trenethyn

Gules, three *Doves* proper, by the
name of *Hodby*.

Hodby.

Ayer.   Azure, 3 *Larks* Or, by the name of *Ayer*.

Argent, three *Owles* Sable, by the
name of *Bridge*.

Bridge.

Sable, three *Owles* Argent, armed Or,
by the name of *Boughton*.   Ar-

Boughton.

Argent, three *Coots* proper, by the name of *Coote*.

Coote.

Parted per *Fess* Argent and Sable, a *Martlet* counterchanged, by the name of *Remis*.

Remis.

Sable, a *Martlet* Argent by the name of *Adam*.

Adam,

Argent, three *Martlets* Gules by the name of *Fornival*.

Fornival.

Azure, three *Martlets* Argent by the name of *Kirketon*.

Kirketon,

Sable, three *Martlets* Argent, by the name of *Naughton*.

Naughton.

Gules, three *Martlets* Argent by the name of *Wotton*.

Wotton.

Per *Cheveron* Or, and Azure, three *Martlets* counterchanged, by the name of *Edgeworth*.

Edgworth.

Sable, four *Martlets*, two and two Argent by the name of *Monter*.

Monster.

Argent, five *Martlets* three and two Gules by the name of *Dowdal*.

Dowdal.

Sable, six *Martlets* 3, 2, 1, by the name of *Apleby*.

Apleby.

Per *Pale Indented* Argent and Sable, six *Martlets* counterchanged, by the name of *Wren*.

Wren.

Sable eight *Martlets* 3, 2, 2, 1, Argent by the name of *Stanton*.

Stanton,

Argent, a *Flower de lis* between eight *Martlets* Sable by the name of *Rochdale*.

Rochdale.

Argent, an *Eſcocheon* within eight *Martlets* Gules, by the name of *Vaux*.

Vaulx.

Gules, a *Creſſent* Ermin between eight *Martlets* Or, by the name of *Bohun*.

Bohun.

Gules, ten *Martlets* 4, 3, 2, 1 Or, by the name of *Tochet*.

Tochet.

Sable, three *Swans* necks couped Argent, by the name of *Squire*.

Squire.

Azure, three *Peacock heads* Erazed Or, by the name of *Beconthorp*.

Beconthorp

Argent, three *Cocks heads* erazed Sable, Membred and *Jolloped* Gules, by the name of *White*.

White.

Gules, two *Wings inverted* and conjoyned Ermine, by the name of *Reney*.

Reny.

Sable, a pair of *Wings* conjoyned, and elevated Argent, born by the Right Honourable *Robert Ridgway* Earl of *Londonderry*, and Barron of *Gallon-Rigeway* in *Ireland*.

*Earl of Lon-
donderry.*

Gules three *Winges* elevated Argent, by the name of *Newport*.

Newport.

Gules three *Wings* pendant Or, by the name of *Baud*.

Baud.

CHAP.

CHAP. VI.

Treats of watry Animals, being such as have their abode, and relief only in the water, to wit Fishes of all sorts, which as they are of a less compleat nature then Earthy, or Aerial Animals, so are they of less esteem in Coat Armour.

As Birds have their Plumes, Wings & Trains for their cutting their passage through the Air; So are Fishes provided with Finns wherewith they guid themselves in their swimming, and cut the current of the streams and waves for their more easie passage wherein their course is directed by their Tayl, as Ships are conducted by their Helm, or Ruther.

Fishes are born after divers manners, viz. directly upright, imbowed, extended, indorsed, respecting each other, surmounting one another. Fretted and Triangle, &c. All Fishes (saith Leigh) that are born feeding shall in Blazon be tearemd devour-
ing,

ing, *and that whereon they feed must be
expressed.*

*All Fishes raised directly upright, and having
Finns must be termed in Blazon Hauriaunt,
signifying to draw, or suck, because that
Fish do oft times put their Heads above
Water to refresh themselves with the cool
Air, but especially when the Waters in
the depth of the Seas do so rage, and as
it were boyl against some Tempestuous
Storm, that they cannot endure the un-
wonted heat thereof, All Fishes being
born transverse, must be Blazoned
Naiant, or Swiming, for in such sort
do they bear themselves in the Water
when they swim.*

*Of Fishes some have hard and crusty Cover-
ings, others a more softer outside, and
these latter are of two sorts, some having
only Skin and others Scales.*

*Fishes are also born in part, and on, or be-
tween, any of the Honourable Ordinaries*

*Of these several kinds, these following Ex-
amples shall suffice.*

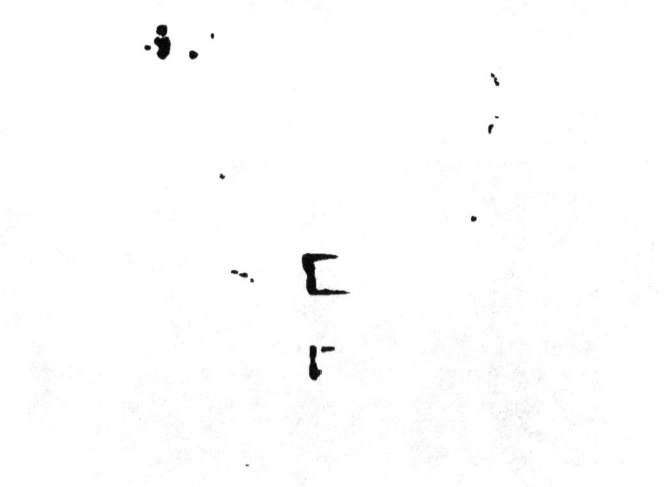

Fish:

Examples of

FISHES.

1. **A**Zure three *Dolphins* Naiant extended in *P le Barry* Or, by the name
of *Dolphin.* The *Dolphin* is here in its natural form of fwiming, and is faid to *Mar-*
fhal their great Troops in admirable order ; for in the *Vaunt-guard* fwim all their
young ones, in the middle the Females,
and in the Rearward all the *Males*, like
good *Husbands* that have a care to their
Wives and *Children.* The *Dolphin* is a
Fifh of fuch great *Strength*, and *Swift-*
nefs, that in his purfuit of other *Fifhes* for
his prey (who make to the *Rocks*, or *Shear*
for *Shelter*) he oft receives danger. The
Naturalift fay that the She *Dolphin* hath
Dugs, and gives fuck to her young. That
the *Dolphin* is a great lover of Mufick,
and loveth the Company of men, but
that

that I leave to the Opinion of the Reader.

2. Sable a *Dolphin* Naiant *Imbowed*, and devouring a Fiſh proper, by the name of *Symonds*.

Symonds.

3. Azure, three *Dolphins hauriant* Or, born by Mr. *Peter Vandeput* of *London* Merchant.

Vandeput.

4 Per *Cheveron* Sable and Argent, in chief two *Dolphins Naiant* reſpecting each other of the ſecond born by *Ambroſe Atfield* Dr. in Divinity; and Vicar of St. *Leonards Shorditch* in *Middleſex.*

Atfield.

5. *Vert*, two *Barbels hauriant* reſpecting each other Argent.

6. Gules, two *Pikes haurlant* endorſed Or.

7. Sable, three *Salmons hauriant* Argent, by the name of *Salmon*.

Salmon.

8. Azure, three *Trouts* fretted in *Triangle teſte ala queve* Argent, by the name of *Trowtheck.*

Trowtheck.

9. Argent, a *Cheveron* Sable, between three *Crevices* upright Gules, theſe are not to be Blazoned *hauriant* as *Fiſhes* that have *Finns* but upright.

10. Argent, a *Lobſters Claw* in Bend ſiniſter Saltire like, ſurmounted of another dexter ways Gules, by the name of *Tregarthick.*

*Tregar-
thick.*

11.

11 Per *Pale* Argent and Gules an *E-scallop* Shell Or, born by Sir *Humphry* Wynch.
Wynch of *Harleford* in Great *Marlow* in *Buckinghamshire*, and of *Hamnes* in *Bedfordshire* Baronet.

12. Topaz, on an *Chief* Diamond, three *Escallop-shells* Pearl; born by the Lord *Preston*, Right Honourable *Richard Grayham*, Viscount *Preston*, and Lord *Graham* of *Eske*, Embassadour for his Majesty King *Charles* the Second to the King of *France*, 1684.

13. Azure, three *Escallops* Or, born by Sir *John Mallet* of St. *Andrews* in West Mallet. *Quantox-head* in *Sommersetshire* Knight.

14. Gules a *Fess dauncette* Or, between three *Escallops* Ermine, born by *Francis Dives* of *Bromham* in *Bedfordshire* Esquire, Dive. Son and Heir of Sir *Lewis Dive* of the said place Knight.

15. Or, two *Barrs* Azure, in *Chief*, three *Escallops* Gules, born by *Edward Clark* of *Chipley* in *Somersetshire* Esquire. Clark.

Sable a *Fess* engrailed between three *Welks* Or, born by Sir *John Shelly* of Shelly. *Michelgrove* in *Sussex* Baronet.

Ex-

Other Examples of Fishes.

Fores.   Gules, a *Dolphin* hauriant Argent, by the name of *Fores.*

Fitz James   Sable, a *Dolphin naiant imbowed* Argent by the name of *Fitz James.*

Visacher.   Gules a *Dolphin naiant* Sable by the name of *Visacher.*

Hanner,   *Vert*, two *Dolphins* indorsed Or, by the name of *Hanner.*

Darburg.   Argent, three *Dolphins naiant* Sable, by the name of *Darburg.*

Pickton.   Argent, three *Pikes* in *Pale* naiant Gules by the name of *Pickton.*

Dolphing-   *Vert*, three *Dolphins naiant* in *Pale* Or,
ley   by the name of *Dolphingley.*

Conghurst.   Azure, three *Congers hauriant* Argent, by the name of *Conghurst.*

Ellis.   Argent, three *Eeles naiant* in *Pale* Barrey Sable, by the name of *Ellis.*

Gesse.   Argent, three *Dog-fishes* naiant in *Pale* Sable, by the name of *Gesse.*

Sea.   *Barry wavey* of six Or and Gules, three *Prawns naiant*, in the first of the second by the name of *Sea*, or *At sea.*

Argent, a *Cheveron engrailed* Sable, between

tween three *Sea Crabs* Gules, by the name of *Bridger*.   *Bridger.*

Argent, an *Escallop* Gules, by the name of *Prelate*.   *Prelate.*

Azure, an *Escallop* Or, by the name of *Bayton*.   *Bayton.*

Gules, three *Escallops* Or, by the name of *Pale*.   *Pale.*

Argent, three *Escallops* Gules by the name of *Barnaby*.   *Barnaby.*

Argent, three *Escallops* Sable by the name of *Strickland*.   *Strickland.*

Sable, three *Escallops* Or, *Walcot*.   *Walcot.*

Azure, three *Esccallops* Or, by the name of *Hartfield*.   *Hartfield.*

Gules, three *Escallops* Or, by the name of *Palmer*.   *Palmer.*

Or, three *Escallops* Gules, by the name of *Harbottle*.   *Harbottle.*

Azure five *Escallops* 2, 2, 1 Argent, by the name of *Rowton*.   *Rowton.*

Azure five *Escallops* 2, 2, 1, Or, by the name of *Shorevile*.   *Shorevile.*

Azure five *Escallops* 2, 1, 2 Or, by the of *Ratesden*.   *Ratesden.*

Azure five *Escallops* 1, 3, 1 Or, by the name of *Barker*.   *Barker.*

Gules, six *Escallops* 3, 2, 1 Argent, by the name of *Scales*.   *Scales.*

N   Sable

Sable six *Escallops* 3, 2, 1 Argent, by the name of *Escot.*

C H A P. VII.

Treats of Monstrous Animals *such as are exorbitant from the general course of Nature either for qualities or essence, and of these there are divers sorts, as Amphibia, that is such as live sometimes as if they were Water Creatures, and other times as if Land Creatures. And those of a more Prodigious Shape, being formed, or rather deformed with the confused Shapes of Creatures of different kinds and qualities, and such are Monsters which St Augustin saith can't be rekoned amongst the good Creatures that God created before the fall of Adam.*

Ex-

Monstruous.Creatures:

Examples of

Monſtruous CREATURES.

1. ARGENT, a *Beaver erected* Sable, devouring a Fiſh, proper.

The *Beaver* hath his Tail only *Fiſh*, which he keeps for the moſt part in the Water, his hinder Leggs are like a Swan, and his foremoſt like a Dogg; ſo he ſwims with the one, whilſt he preyeth with the other.

2. Argent a *Feſs* between three *Otters* Sable, born by *Symon Lutterel* of *Lutterel* in the County of *Dublin* in *Ireland* Eſquire. It is reported that in *China* they train up *Otters* as we do *Spaniels* which go into the Water and bring forth Fiſh at the command of their Maſters, which cuſtome hath been practiſed of late years by ſome in *England*.

Lutterel.

N 2   3. Azure

3. Azure, a *Musimon* Argent.

This is a *Bigenerous* Beast of an un-kindly procreation being engendred between a *Goat* and a *Ram*; like as *Tyterus* is between an *Ewe* and a *BuckGoat*.

4. Gules, a *Leopard passant* gardant, Or, spotted Sable.

The Shape of the *Leopard* denoteth his unkindly Birth, and to be degenerate from the *Lyon*, but more agreeable to the *Pardus* in his shape and spots; nor hath he the noble Courage of the *Lyon*, to whom he is a mortal Enemy, and oft times by his subtle, treacherous policy doth get him into a Snare.

5. Argent, on a Cross Sable a *Leopards face* Or, born by *George Rodeney Bridges* of *Keynsham* in *Somersetshire*, Esquire. One of the Grooms of the Bedchamber to his Majesty King *Charles* the Second.

Bridges

6. Diamond, a *Cheveron* between three *Leopards heads* or *Faces* Topaz by the name of *Wentworth*.

Wentworth.   This with a Garter is born by the Right Honourable *William* Earl of *Strafford*, Viscount *Wentworth*, Baron of *Wentworth Woodhouse*, *Newmarch*, *Oversley* and *Rabby*, Knight of the *Garter*, &c.

Earl of Strafford.

This Coat with a due difference is born
by

by Sir *William Wentworth* of *Wakefield* Kt.
By *Jo.Wentworth* of *North Empfal* Knight.
By *Jo Wentworth* of *Wolley* Efquire, and
by *John Wentworth* of *Elmfhel* Efquire, all
of the *Weft Riding* of *Yorkfhire*.

Pearl, a *Cheveron* Ruby between three *Leopards Faces* Diamond, born by the Right Honourable *Francis* Vifcount *Newport* of *Bradford*, Baron *Newport* of *High Ercall*, Lord Leiutenant of *Shropfhire*, Treafurer of his Majefties Houfhold, and one of the Lords of his Majefties moft Honourable Privy Counfel, *&c.*

Or, a Cheveron between three *Leopards faces* Sable, born by Sir *Charles Wheeler* of *Burbury* in *Warwickfhire* Baronet, antiently of *Martin Huffingftre* in *Worcefterfhire*.

Vert, a *Cheveron* between three *Leopards faces* Or, born by Sir *Thomas Fitch* of *Eltham*, and *Mount Mafcal* in Kent Knight.

Sable, a *Cheveron* between three *Leopards faces* Argent, born by Mr. *Thomas Hawes* of *London* Merchant.

7. Argent on a *Bend engrailed* Gules, three *Leopards faces* Or, born by *Nicho-as Barbon* of *London* M. D. and one

Lord Vif-
count
Newport.

Wheeler.

Fitch.

Hawes.

Barbon.

N 3　　　　of

of the Colledge of *Physitians* of *Lon-don.*

8. Sable, two Barrs Ermin, in *Chief* three *Leopards faces* Or, born by *Owen Feltham* of *Grais Inn* in *Middlesex* Esquire.

Feltham.

9. Gules on a *Bend* Argent, three *Leopards faces* of the field, born by Collonel *Robert Werden* of *Chester*, Comptroler to the Houshold of his *Royal Highness* James *Duke* of *York*, and first *Lieutenant* and *Major* of his Guards.

VVerden.

Or, on a *Bend* Azure, three *Leopards faces* Argent, born by *Jo. Mingay* of *Ginninham* in *Norfolk* Esquire.

Mingay.

10. Gules a *Cheveron* between two *Leopards faces* in Chief, a *Bugle horn* in Base Argent, born by Sir *Thomas Slingsby* of *Skriven* in the West Riding of *Yorkshire* Baronet.

Slingsby.

11. Sable a *Leopards head* Argent, *Jessant* a *Flower de lis* Or, born by Sir *William Morley* of *Halnaker* in *Sussex* Knight of the Bath.

Morley.

12. Argent a *Cheveron* between three *Seals feet* erected, and erazed Sable, These Arms belongs to the Town of *Yarmouth* in *Norfolk.*

The

Monstruous Creatures.

.The *Milk* of the *Seal* is said to be very good against the falling Sickness.

***

Other Examples of

Monstruous CREATURES.

1. **A**Zure, a *Griffon passant*, and a *Chief* Or, born by *George Evelyn* of *Godstone*, and *Ditton* in *Surrey* Esquire, And by *John Evelyn* of *Sayes Court* near *Deptford* in *Kent* Esquire. *Evelyn.*

2. Ermine, a *Griffon Segreant*, or Rampant Saphir, born by the Right Honorable *Francis* Lord *Aungier*, Earl, Viscount, and Baron of *Longford* in *Ireland*, and one of the *Lords* of his Mjesties most Honourable *Privy Councel* for that Kingdom, *&c.*

Sable, a *Griffon Segreant* Or *Rampant* Argent, born by *Edward Griffin* of *Dingley* in *Northamptonshire* Esquire, *Treasurer*

of

of the *Chamber* to his *Majesty* King *Charles* the Second, and *Leiutenant Collorel* of his *Majesties* own *Troop* of *Horse-Guards.*

Read.
Corselis.
Azure, a *Griffon Segreant* Or, by the name of *Read.* This Coat is also born by Mr. *James Corsellis* of *London* Merchant.

Meverell.
Argent, a *Griffon Segreant* Or, born by *Owen Meverell* Doctor of Physick.

Coling.
Azure, a *Griffon Segreant* Sable, born by *Richard Coling* of *Coreley* in *Shropshire* Esquire, principal *Secretary* to the Earl of *Arlington,* Lord *Chamberlain* of his *Majesties* houshold.

Hawkins.
3. Or, on a *Cheveron* between three *Cinquefoils* Azure, as many *Escollops* Argent, on a cheif Gules, a *Griffon Passant* of the Third, born by *Richard Hawkins* of *Marsham* in *Berkshire* Esquire.

Williams.
4. Argent, a *Dragons-head erazed* Vert, *holding* in his mouth a *finister hand couped* at the wrist Gules, born by Sir *John Williams* of *Muftow house* in *Fulham* in *Middlesex* Knight, Son and Heir of Sir *Thomas Williams* of *Eltham Court* in *Kent* Knight and Baronet.

Dashwood.
5. Argent, on a *Fess* between a *double Cottize* Gules, three *Griffons heads* erazed Or, born by Sir *Robert Dashwood* of *Norbrook,* and *Wickham* in *Oxfordshire* Knight.   6. Sable

6. Sable, a *Cheveron* between three *Griffons* heads erazed Argent, born by Sir *John Cotton* of *Lanwade* of *Cambridgshire* Baronet.

7. Argent, a *Wivern* his *Wings* displayed, and Tail nowed Gules, by the name of *Drakes.*

Like as the *Griffin* doth pertake of a *Fowl*, to wit an *Eagle* in the fore-part and a *Lion* in the hinder, so doth the *Wivern* in the fore-part the Wings and Legs of a *Fowl*, and of an *Adder, Snake,* or *Serpent* in the *Tail.*

8. Sable, a *Cockatrice* displayed Argent, *Crested, Membred,* and *Jolloped* Gules.

The *Cockatrice* is of that pestiferous, and poysonous quality that he is termed the King of *Serpents.*

9 Azure, a *Harpey* with her Wings disclosed, and her Hair flotant Or, This Coat stands in the Church at *Huntington.*

10. Argent, a *Mearemaid* Gules, crined Or, holding in her right hand a *Mirror,* and in her left a *Comb,* by the name of *Ellis.*

11. Or, a *Dragon* Passant Vert.

12. Argent, a *Reremouse* or *Bat* displayed

Bakster.　played Sable, by the name of *Bakster.*

The *Reremouse* doth pertake both with the *Beast* and *Bird,* so that it can't be well said to which it doth belong; for by her *Wings* and *Flying* she should be a *Bird,* and by her body a kind of a *Mouse.* She bringeth forth her young, and suckleth them with her *Paps* which *Birds* do not.

Under this head cometh *Montegres, Satyres, Monk-fishes,* as also *Lion-dragons, Lions-poisons,* and all other double shaped *Animals.*

CHAP.

CHAP. VIII.

Having in these foregoing Chap-
ters treated of the who'e Body
of Heraldry, *with* Rules *and* Ex-
amples sufficient to blazon any
Coat Armour ; *my next business*
shall be to lay down some few Rules
for the Marshalling *and* Impaling
of Coats *in one* Shield.

BY *Marshalling* of *Coats* is to be
underftood an orderly difpo-
fing of fundry *Coat Armours*
pertaining to diftinct Families,
and of their contingent *Ornaments* with
their *Parts* and *Appurtenances* in their proper places. And of thefe fome have
their place within the *Efcocheon*, and fome
without : of thofe within fome have their
occafions obfcure, and others manifeft,
as are thofe whofe *Marshalling* (according

Marshal-
ing of
Coats.

ing to ancient and prescript forms) do apparently betoken *Marriage*, or some gift of the *Soveraign*. Such as betoken *Marriage* do represent either a *Match* single, or *Hereditary*: By a single *Match*, is meant the conjoyning the *Coat Armour* of the *Man* with the *Woman* which is *Impaled* on the sinister side of the Mans; but if she be an *Heiress* then her *Coat* is to be born in an *Escocheon* of *Pretence* in the midst of his *Shield*, and over the *Charge*, if there charged.

It is also accustomary for *Bishops* to *Impale* on the dexter side of their *Coats*, the *Coat* belonging to their *Episcopal See*.

And if a *Man* hath had more than one Wife, the way of Bearing them is to *Impale* them betwixt his own, which is to be in the middle part of the *Shield*, Examples of all which shall be given for the Readers better instructions therein.

He

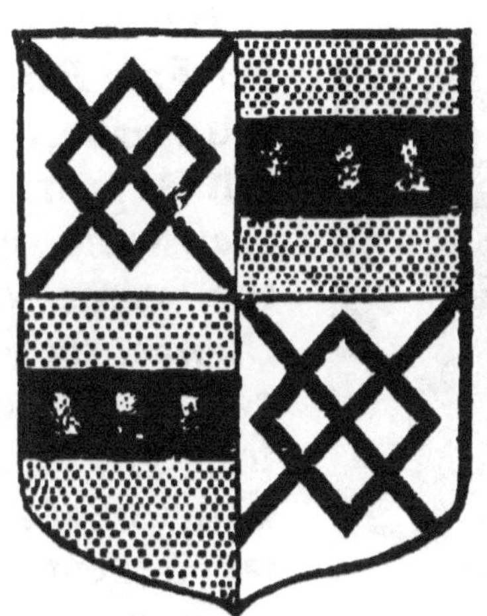

He Beareth, two Coats quarterly both by the name of *Vernon*, 1. Argent, a *Frett* Sable, 2*dly.* Or on a *Fess* Azure, three *Garbs* Or, the 3*d.* as the 2*d.* the 4*th.* as firſt. Theſe *Coats*

thus Marſhalled are born by *George Vernon* of *Sudbury* in *Derbyſhire*, and of *Haſlington* in *Cheſhire* Eſquire, deſcended of the *Vernons* who were anciently *Barons* of *Shibbrook* in the ſaid County of *Cheſter.*

After this manner are a greater number of *Quarterings* born, as will appear by the Examples given in the Second Part.

Clayton.

He Beareth Per Pale *Baron* and *Femme*, the firſt Argent, a *Croſs* Sable, by the name of *Clayton*, the ſecond *Paly* of ſix Or, and Gules, on a *Canton* Argent, a *Bear* rampant Sable, by the name of *Trot*.

Theſe *Coats* are thus born by Sir *Robert Clayton* of *Marden* in *Surry*, and of the City of *London* Knight and *Alderman*, Lord *Mayor* thereof *Anno* 1680, who is now Married to *Martha* Eldeſt Daughter of *Perient Trot* of *London* Merchant.

He Beareth Baron, Impaled between his two *Wives*, first in the midst Ruby a Bezant between three Demy Lions Rampant Pearl by the name of *Bennet*. Lord Of-*westre.*

2*dly.* On the dexter fide Topaz on a *Pallet* Saphir, three *Flower de lis* of the Field, being the Coat of *Elizabeth* Countefs of *Mulgrave*, and Daughter to the Earl of *Middlefex* firft Wife to the bearer hereof.

3*dly.* On the finifter fide Topaz, a *Fefs* between three *Wolves heads* couped Diamond, born by *Bridget How* of the Family of Sir *Grubham How* prefent Wife to the bearer hereof the Right Honourable Sir *John Bennet* Knight of the Bath, and Baron *Bennet* of *Ofweftre* in *Middlefex*.

He

He Beareth
Azure, a *Wheat
Sheaf* Or *Garb*
Or, by the
name of *Gros-
venor*, in an Es-
cocheon of Pre-
tence the Arms
of *Davies* viz.
Or a *Cheveron*
between three
Mullets pier-
ced Sable ; this with the Arms of *Ulster*
is the Bearing of Sir *Thomas Grosvenor* of
Eaton in *Cheshire* Baronet, now Married
to *Mary* sole Daughter and Heir to *A-
lexander Davies* of the *Mill-Bank* in the
Parish of Saint *Margarets Westminster* in
Middlesex Esquire.

He Beareth quarterly, firſt Argent, a *Lion* rampant Gules between three *Pheons* Sable, by the name of *Egerton.*

2. Barry of ſix Argent, and Azure, in Cheif three *Torte-auxes*, a *File* Ermine, by the name of *Grey.*

3. Sable, on a Bend between two *Cot-tizes* Argent, a *Roſe* Gules between two *Amulets* of the Field, by the name of *Con-way.* the 4*th.* as the firſt on an *Eſcocheon* of *Pretence,* Gules, two Helmets in chief Ar-gent, and a *Wheat Sheaf* in baſe Or, by the name of *Cholmeley.* Theſe Coats are thus born by *John Egerton* of *Broxton* in *Cheſhire* Eſquire, eldeſt Son of Sir *Philip Egerton* of *Egerton,* and *Oxton* in the ſaid County Knight, which *John* is now Married to the Daughter and Co-heir of *Tho. Cholmeley* or *Cholmondley* oſ *Vale Roy-al* in *Cheſhi e* Eſquire.

Werden.

He Beareth
Gules on a
Bend Argent,
three *Leopards*
heads *Or,* faces
of the Field by
the Name of
Werden, Im-
paled with *Sa-*
ble, a *Cross* en-
grailed between
four *Crescents*
Argent, in right of *Jane* Daughter of
Edward Barnham of *Cockhall* in *Kent* Esq;
first Wife to the bearer hereof ; and in an
Escocheon of Pretence Sable, two Swords
Saltierwise with their points downwards Argent, Pomeled and Hilted *Or,*
by the name of *Towse,* in right of *Mar-*
garet Daughter and Heir of *William*
Towse of *Basingborn-hall* in *Essex* Esquire,
present Wife to the bearer hereof
Collonel *Robert Werden* of *Chester,* Comp-
troller of the house of his Royal *High-*
ness James Duke of *York,* and first *Leiu-*
tenant, and *Major* of his *Guards.*

    This Example sheweth how a *Man*
should Bear the *Arms* of his *Wives* the

one

one being an *Heiress*, and the other not. The other *Examples* shew how the *Coats* of the *Wives* are to be born.

Having given examples of the *Marshalling* of *Quarterings*, *Impalings*, and *Escocheons* of *Pretence* for *Wives*. In the next place I shall treat of *Augmentations* of honour bestowed on the *Bearer* by his Sovereign for Favour or Merit, and of these some are *Impaled* with their *Paternal Coats*, and others born only on a *Canton*, *Quarter*, or *Chief*.

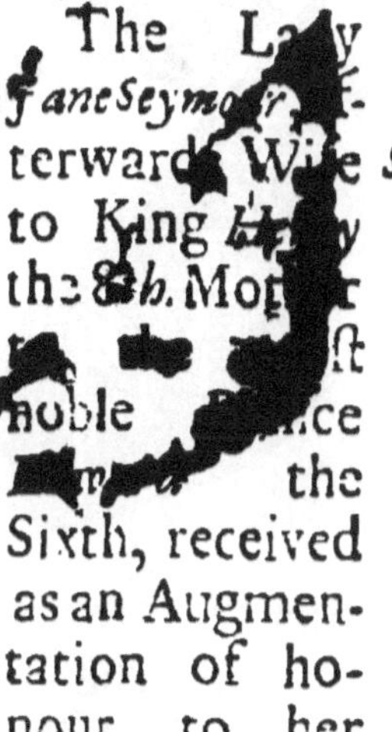

The Lady *Jane Seymour* afterwards Wife to King Henry the 8*th*. Mother to that most noble Prince King Edward the Sixth, received as an Augmentation of honour to her

Seymour.

nour to her Family by the gift of her said Husband these *Arms* born on the dexter side of of the *Escocheon*, viz *Sol*, on a *Pile Mars*, between six *Flower de lis*, *Jupiter*, three

Lions

Lions Passant Gardant of the first, *Impaled* with her Paternal Coat, viz. *Mars* two *Wings Pale ways* inverted, Or two *Wings* in *Lure Sol*. This Coat is now born by the Right Noble *Charles Seymour*, Duke of *Somerset*, Marquess and Earl of *Hertford*, Viscount *Beauchamp*, *Baron Seymour*, and Knight of the most noble Order of the Garter.

Ruby, on a *Bend* between six *Cross Croslets Flichee* Pearl, an *Escocheon* Topaz, thereon a *Demy Lion* peirced through the mouth with an *Arrow*, within a double Treasure counter-floured of the first: and is the Paternal Coat of the Right Noble and ancient Family of the *Howards*, which now flourisheth in the persons of his Grace *Henry* Duke of *Norfolk*, Earl of *Arundel*, *Surrey*, *Norfolk*, and *Norwich*, Baron *Howard*, *Fitz-Alan*, *Matravers*,

Duke of Norfolk.

Maw-

Mawbrey, Segrave, Bruce, Clun, Oswald-Stre, and *Castle Rising,* Earl *Marshal* of *England,* Constable of *Windsor Castle,* &c.

The Right Honourable *James* Earl of *Suffolk,* Baron *Howard* of *Walden.*   Earl of Suffolk.

The Right Honourable *Thomas* Earl of *Berkshire,* Viscount *Andover,* and Baron *Howard* of *Charlton.*   Earl of Berk-shire.

The Right Honourable *Charles* Earl of *Carlisle,* Viscount *Howard* of *Morpeth,* Baron *Dacres* of *Gisland,* Lord Leiute-nant of the Counties of *Cumberland* and *Westmoreland, Vice-Admiral* of the *Coasts* of *Northumberland, Cumberland, Westmore-land, Durham,* and Maritine parts adjacent.   Earl of Carlislo.

The Right Honourable *William* Ho-ward Viscount aud Baron *Stafford, An-no* 1680.   Lord staf-ford.

The Right Honourable *William* Lord *Howard,* Baron of *Escrick.*   Lord Ho-ward.

The Honourable *Charles Howard* of *Graftock* in *Cumberland* Esquire, brother to his Grace *Henry* late Duke of *Norfolk.*   Charles Howard Esq;

The Honourable Sir *Robert Howard* of *Vastern* in *Wiltshire* Knight, Brother to the Right Honourable *Thomas* Earl of *Berk-shire*   Sir Robert Howard.

And the Honourable Sir *Philip Howard* Knight, Captain of the *Queens Troop* of   Sir Phillip Howard.

his

his *Majesties Guards*, and Brother to the Right Honourable *Charles* Earl of *Carlisle*. And from these and their *Ancestors* Loins, have issued forth divers worthy Gentlemen as Stems to support the Dignity of the said Family.

The said *Augmentation* on the *Bend* was Granted unto the Right noble *Thomas* Duke of *Norfolk* and his descendants by King *Henry* the eigth, for his signal Service as General of the Army which gave that remarkable overthrow at *Floding* to King *James* the forth of *Scotland* ; which said *Duke* was by King *Henry* the *Seventh* created Knight of the *Garter*, and made Lord *High Treasurer of England*.

To all the Arms of all *Baronets* King *James* granted according to the first Institution of that degree as an Augmentation of honour to them and their descendants the Arms of *Ulster*, viz. a sinister *Hand* couped at the Wrist Gules, to be born in a *Canton* or *Escocheon* Argent, which said *Augmentation* is placed in the most convenientest place of the Shield.

The

The *Field* is Topaz, two *Bars* Saphir, a cheif *quarterly Jupiter* and *Mars* on the first two *Flower de lis Sol*, on the second a *Lion Paſſant Gardant* of the laſt; the third as the second, the fourth as the firſt. This Coat belongs to the Right Honourable *John Mannors*, Earl of *Rutland*, Baron *Roſs* of *Hamlake*, *Trusbut*, and *Belvoyr*, which was given in *Augmentation* to this Family, being descended of the Blood Royal from King *Edward* the *Fourth*.

Earl of *Rutland*.

O 4   CHAP.

CHAP. IX.

In the former Chapters *have been treated of such things in* Coat Armour *as are within the* Shield *or* Escocheon ; *I shall now treat of those external* Ornaments *without the* Escocheon, *viz.* Helmets, Torces, *or* Wreaths, Caps, Crowns, Crests, Mantlings, *and* Escroles : *and to* Noble Men Supporters; *of all which in order.*

THE *Helmet* is placed next above the *Escocheon* or *Shield* to all under the degree of a *Noble Man,* And to the Nobility there is a *Crown,* and the *Helmet* issuing out of the said *Crown.*

The *Helmet* doth distinguish the dignity of the *Bearer,* for to a *Gentleman* and an an *Esquire* the *Helmet* is placed sideways with the *Bever* close.

To a *Knight*, or *Baronet* (which is all one) the *Helmet* is placed foreright with the *Bever* open. The full faced *Helmet* doth signifie direction and command, the close attention and obedience.

The open *Helmet* placed sideways with Bars doth belong to all *Nobles* under the *Degree* of his Majesty, and Sovereign *Dukes*, or those of the *Blood Royal*.

To *Kings, Sovereign Princes* and *Dukes* of the Royal Blood the *Helmet* is placed foreright with open *Bars*; all which will appear in the second Part of this *Book* in the *Chapters* relating to that *Degree* they are of; as will the *Crowns* or *Coronets* by which each *Degree* of the *Nobility* are distinguished.

Coronets.

The *Barons Coronet* is with six *Pearls* of an equal height, and distance one from the other.

The *Viscounts Coronet* is composed only of *Pearls* close set together and of an equal height without *Flowers* or *Points*.

An

Earls Co-
ronet.

An *Earls Coronet* is compoſed of *Points* and *Flowers*, but the *Points* are *Spiry* with *Pearls* on the top above the *Flowers.*

Marqueſs.
Coronet.

The *Coronet* of a *Marquis* is of *Leaves*, and *Points*, with the *Leaves* and *Flowers* above the *Points.*

Dukes Co-
ronet.

The *Coronet* of a *Duke* is only *Floral.*

Princes
Coronet.

The *Coronet* of a *Prince* is the ſame with the Crown of a King, only the *Arches, Mound,* and *Croſs* are wanting.

The Crown of a King is as a Dukes, but with *Arches, Mound,* and *Croſs.*

To a *Biſhop* inſtead of a *Coronet* doth belong a *Miter.*

Torce or
VVreath.

Next above the *Helmet* is the *Wreath* or *Torce* which is of the principal *Metal* and *Colour* in the *Bearers Paternal Coat,* this the Creſt ſtands upon : beſides which it oft times ſtands upon a *Mount, Hill, Chapeau,* Or *Coronet.*

Creſts.

Creſts are various each Family having one appropriate to themſelves. About the *Shield* reaching from the top of the *Helmet* to the bottom of the *Shield* is

Mantle.

the *Mantle* which is to cover or wrap about the ſame. And theſe *Mantlings* are of a different ſhape, and compoſure, and at the will of the *Bearer* to be altered at pleaſure, thoſe commonly made uſe of

are

are the *Cloak Mantles* (antiently ufed)
and the *Folding Mantles.*

On each fide of the *Shield* are placed
Supporters for *Noble Men.* *Supporters.*

The *Efcrole* is at the bottom of the
Shield in which is placed the *Motto* Or
Device of the *Bearer* which is according
to his Fancy, and may be altered at pleafure, but moft commonly it alludes to the
Coat, *Creft,* *Name,* or Imploy. And on
the *Efcrole* ftands the *Supporters.*

The End of the Firft Part.

HO-

HONOUR CIVIL

ACCORDING TO THE

LAWS of ENGLAND.

With *Examples* of the *Atchive-ments* of each *Degree* of *Honour*: And for the better explanation thereof one *Example* of each *Degree* is *Blazoned*: Which method is to be obferved to all others.

The Second Part.

CHAP. X.

As in Mans Body for the prefervation of the whole, divers Functions and Offices of Members are required, even fo in

all

all well governed Kingdomes *a diſtin-*
ĉtion of perſons is neceſſary, and the
policy of England is ſuch to have made
a threefold diviſion of perſons, firſt the
King, *under which name a Soveraign*
Queen is compriſed, Secondly the Nobles, *viz. the* Prince, Dukes, Mar- *Degrees of*
queſſes, Earls, Viſcounts, *and* Lords *Honour.*
Spiritual *and* Temporal, *and Thirdly*
the Commons *which comprehends* Baronets, Knights, Eſquires, *and* Gentlemen, *&c.*

Our *Laws* contrary to other *Coun-*
treys calls Noble under the degree of a
Lord, and the *Nobility* are *Peers* of the
Realm, and do ſit together in the *Kings*
great *Councel* of Parliament with his Majeſty, and the word *Nobility* or *Noble* ſignifies to expreſs men of generoſity of
blood and *degree,* as alſo the Reward of
Vertue, but a word or two of each Degree in particular, and firſt of the King
the Fountain from whom all *Rivulets* and
ſwelling Streams of Honour ſpring
Of the King or Monarch of Great Brittain.

Monarchy is as ancient as Man, *Adam*
being created Soveraign Lord of the U-
niverſe, whoſe Office was to govern the
World, and all Creatures therein, his Po-
ſterity

sterity divided into *Tribes*, and *Generations* acknowledged no other dominion then Paternity and Eldership, till men and vice multiplying, pride and violence adumbrated filial Piety, and obedience, the powerful oppreffing the feble; which neceffitated the introduction of a Politick Government, and put an end to the good old Age; the moft valiant Stems, or Nations electing to themfelves *Kings* to command them in peace, and to lead them forth to battle, which the *Greeks* call *Monarches*; others became governed under a felect number of Majeftrates which is called *Ariftocracy*, and others were fo unfortunate as to fall under the yoke of *Democracy*.

The Ifland of *Great Brittain ab Origine* owned a Regal Power as *Cæfars Commentaries*, and all our Chronicles fets forth.

The *Brittains* were at firft divided into many Kingdoms; which afterwards were contracted into two *Monarchies*, *viz.* the *Englifh* and the *Scots*, and in the end united into one, and the ancient name of *Great Brittain* reftored in *King James* as the right Heir and Defcendant of the *Brittifh Saxon*, *Danifh*, *Norman*, and *Scottifh Kings*, from whom it defcended to our immediate Soveraign King

Charles

Charles the Second, in whose Veins all those Soveraign Streams of Royal Blood are conjoined to Unite those jarring Nations into one Body under a Head unto which each one may justly claim an interest.

The King is Gods *Vice-Gerent*, and ought to be obeyed; if good he is a blessing, if bad a judgment, against whom we are to use no other Weapons but *Prayers* and *Tears* for his amendment, he is stiled *Pater Patria* and because the protection of his Subjects belongs to his care, the *Militia* is annexed to his Crown that the *Sword* and *Scepter* may be both in his hand.

It is the manner for Kings to Write in the Plural number, which is Gods own stile, *Mandamus*, *Volumus*, &c. And the Scripture calls them *Gods*, in which sence they may be stiled *Divi*, or *Dij*, *quia Vicarij*, & *Dei voce indicat* : And our *Lawyers* say, *Rex est persona mixta cum sacerdote*, which denotes his Power in *Causes Ecclesiastical*.

The *Ceremonies* at the Coronation are many, and more solemn with us, then in many other Countries, as the anointing with *Oyl*, an *Imperial Crown* set on his head

(which

(which is always done by the *Arch-Bishop* of *Canterbury*, as a Prerogative belonging to that *See*) A *Scepter* the ancient Ensign of Regality is put into his hand to signifie Juftice, a *Ring* is put on his Finger to denote Faithfulnefs; a *Sword* for Vengeance, and a *Mound* that is a *Globe* Crefted with a Crofs put in his right hand, the *Globe* denoting his Dominions by *Sea* and *Land*, and the Crofs his Faith.

The Kings Office. The Office of the King of *England* according to *Fortefcue* is to fight the Battles of his People, and to do them Right and *Juftice*. To enable him to perform this weighty office certain *Powers* and *Priviledges* are allowed him by the Law of the Land, amongft which he hath the power of the *Militia* both by *Land* and *Sea*, of making Peace and War, he hath all ftrong holds as *Caftles*, *Forts* and the like; he hath the power of *calling*, *adjourning*, *proroging*, and *diffolving Parliaments* at pleafure; alfo the encreafing the number of the Members of both *Houfes* by creating new *Peers*, or beftowing new Priviledges to *Boroughs*, to elect and fend *Burgeffes* by his Writ to *Parliament*.

The *Bills* that pafs both Houfes receive the name of *Laws* from his breath, and

are

are annihilated if he lays them by without giving a reason for it. He hath the sole nomination of all *Commanders* and *Offices* both *Military, Civil, and Ecclesiastical*, the power of conferring Honours, dispencing with *Penal Statutes*, the pardoning of *Criminals* the Coyning of *Money*, the erecting and making *Cities, Universities, Colledges, Hospitals, Fairs, Markets, Forrests, Chafes*, &c. The Enfranchising of *Aliens*, the granting of *Letters of Mart*: he hath the regulation of *Weights*, and *Measures*, and the setting of prizes on *Provisions* within the *Verge* of his *Court*, which is twelve Miles round, which said office is executed by his *Clerk* of the *Markets* for the said *Verge*; he hath also the power to take *Carts, Wagons*, or *Boats* for the carrying his Goods from one *Palace* to another paying the Rates allowed by the *Statute*.

And for declaring his Royal pleasure he issueth forth his *Proclamations* which ought to be strictly obeyed by all his *Subjects*.

Debts due to the King are first to be satisfied, and all *Receivers* of his *Money* and *Revenues*, their *Persons Lands, Goods, Heirs, Executors* &c. are at all times

P

chargeable

chargeable for the same, for *Nullum tempus occurit Regi.*

In doubtful cases no Statute restrains the King unless he be especially named therein, no *Estoppel* can bind him, no *Judgment* final in a *Writ* of Right *Judgments* entred against him are with *Salvo jure domini Regis.*

The King hath the Custody of all *Idiots* and *Lunaticks*; to him belongs all Estates for want of Heirs, by *Forfeitures, Escheats,* &c.

All *Treasure, Trove,* all *Waifs, Estrais, Wrecks,* at Sea and the like not granted from the Crown belongs to him, the like doth all waste *Lands, Gold,* and *Silver Mines,* the Royalties of *Hawking, Hunting, Fishing,* and *Fowling.*

In the Church his *Prerogative* Power is very great, he can call *National Synods* for the making of *Canons* for the introducing of Ceremonies into the Church to reform *Heresies, Schism* and the like.

He hath the Patronage of all *Bishopricks* and the making of all *Bishops.*

These with many other are the Prerogatives that belongs to the Crown of *England.*

The

HONI · SOIT · QVI · MAL · Y · PENSE
DIEU
DROIT
Atchivement of his Sacred Ma.tie
King Charles the 2d. &c.a

The ATCHIEVEMENT
of the KING.

THe *Royal Atchievement;* or *Armorial Ensign of Honour* belonging to His *Majesty* is as followeth, Quarterly quartered first *Jupiter* three *Flowers de lis Sol,* quartered with *Mars* three *Lions passant-Gardant* in pale *Sol.* 2dly, *Sol* within a double *Tresure counter flowred* a *Lion Rampant Mars.* 3dly, *Jupiter* an *Irish harp Sol,* stringed *Luna,* the fourth and last quarter in all points as the first, all within the *Royal Garter,* on a *Helmet* adorned with an Imperial *Crown,* a *Lion passant Gardant* crowned *Sol,* mantled with *Cloth of Gold,* lined *Ermine, supported* on the dexter side with a *Lion Gardant* crowned *Sol* and on the sinister with an *Unicorn Luna* thereto a *Chein* reflexed over his back, and a field *Sol* and in a Compartment beareth his Motto *DIEV ET MON DROIT.*

                    Of

Of the PRINCE.

THe Kings eldest Son (who is Heir apparent from the day of his Birth) is entituled Prince, from the Latin word *quasi principalis post Regem.*

See Guil.
lm Second
part Chap-
ter 3.

Prince of
Wales.
    The first that is read of in *England* was *Edward* eldest Son to King *Henry* the Third, since which time the eldest Son of the King hath been by Patent, and other Ceremonies Created *Prince* of *Wales*, Earl of *Chester*, and *Flint*, &c.

King *Edward* the Third added the Dukedome of *Cornwal* with the said Principality, and made the Black Prince his Son Prince of *Aquitane*, and since the Union of *Scotland* his Title hath been *Princeps Mag. Brittania*, but ordinarily Prince of *Wales*. As eldest Son to the King of *Scotland* he is Duke of *Rothsay*, and *Seneschal* of *Scotland* from his birth, and so long as *Normandy* remained in the Kings possession he was stiled Duke of *Province.*

At his Creation he is presented before the King in *Princely Robes*, who puts a *Co-*

ronet

ronet on his head, a *Ring* on his middle *Finger*, and a Verge of Gold into his hand, as also his *Letters Patents* after they are read.

The *Mantle* that he wears in *Parliament* is once more doubled upon the Shoulder then a *Dukes*, his *Cap* of State indented. his *Coronet* formerly of *Croffes* and *Flower de lis*, but hath now an *Arch* added, with a *Ball* and *Crofs* in the midft on the *Summit*, by order of his prefent Majefty King *Charles* the Second. And the *Coronet* with *Croffes* and *Flower de lis* was then allowed to his *Royal Highnefs James* Duke of *York*; and all immediate Sons and Brothers of the Kings of *England*, but their Sons although they hold the Titles of Dukes are to ufe the *Coronet* of Leaves only as other *Dukes* do.

The Prince is a diftinct Perfon from the King, he is a Subject, and holds his Principalities of the King, and is fubject to the Law, in token of which fubjection he ufeth this Pofie *ICH DIEV* an old *Saxon* word which fignifies *I Serve*, which is placed about a *Flower de lis*.

 DUKES.

DUKES.

A Duke is called *Dux a ducendo* from being a *General* or *Leader* of an Army, but of late days this dignity is given by the King to men of *Blood* and Merit by *Patent*. And the first English *Duke* was *Edward* the *Black Prince* who was created Duke of *Cornwal* by his Father *Edward* the *Third*.

Chapron. Their *Chapron*, or head *attire* is of *Scarlet* doubled Ermine ; their *Coronet* made of *Strawberry Leaves*, his Mantle guarded with four Guards, he holds a Verge of Gold in his hand, and at his Creation hath his *Sword* put over his Shoulders, or guided to him which Viscounts, and *Barons* have not.

Dukes Privi- ledges. He may in all places out of the *Kings* or *Princes* presence erect his Cloth of *Estate* hanging down within half a yard of the Ground ; his *Dutchess* may have her Train born up by a *Baroness*, and no *Earl* without his permission is to wash with him.

By Curtesie all *Dukes* eldest Sons are
stiled

FORTIER FIDELIER FOELICITER
Atchivement of his Grace Chris=
=topher Duke of Albemarle &c.ª

ſtiled Marqueſſes, and the younger Lords, and take place of Viſcounts; he hath that Title of Grace, and is ſtiled moſt potent, and noble Prince.

Dukes of the Blood Royal are ſtiled, moſt High, Mighty, and Illuſtrious Princes.

The Kings younger Sons are ſtiled Princes, by Birth, but have their Titles of Dukes, Marqueſſes, &c. from Creation.

The Daughters are ſtiled Princeſſes, and the Title of Royal Highneſs is due to them all both Sons and Daughters.

I ſhall give you for example of the Bearing of a Duke the Atchievement of his Grace Chriſtopher Duke of Albemarle.

Atchievement of the Duke of Albemarle.

The Right Noble Chriſtopher Duke of Albemarle, Earl of Torrington, Baron Monk of Potheridge, Beauchamp, and Teys Knight of the moſt noble Order of the Garter, Lord Leiutenant of Eſſex and Devonſhire, Captain of his Majeſties Life Guards and Guards of Horſe, one of the Gentlemen of his Bed-chamber, and one of the Lords of his moſt Honourable Privy Councel, &c. Beareth within a Garter, Ruby a Cheveron between three Lions heads erazed Pearl, Enſigned with a Coronet, and Helmet be-

ſitting

sitting his Graces quality, thereon on a Cheapeau *Ruby,* lined *Ermine* a *Cat-a-Mountain* passant per Pale *Diamond* and *Pearl* between two *Palm* branches proper; mantled *Ruby,* double *Ermine* ; supported on the dexter side by a Lion, and on the sinister by a *Griffon* both Pearl, and holding on their *Shoulders* a *Palm Branch* proper ; and for his *Motto* in a Scrole FORTIER : FIDELITER FOELICITER.

MARQUISSES.

A *Marquiss* according to the *Saxon* word *Markenreve* signifies a Governour of the *Marches* ; he hath the next place of Honour to a *Duke* ; he is Created by girding on a *Sword,* by puting on his *Head* a *Chaplet* of Gold, and delivering into his hand a *Patent* under the great Seal for the said *Dignity,* his *Coronet* is partly *Flowred,* and partly *Pyramidal,* his *Mantle* and *Cheapeau* is *Crimson* or *Scarlet,* doubled Ermine, with three *guards* and a half on the *Shoulders* ; his Title is most Noble and Honourable *Prince.*   In the

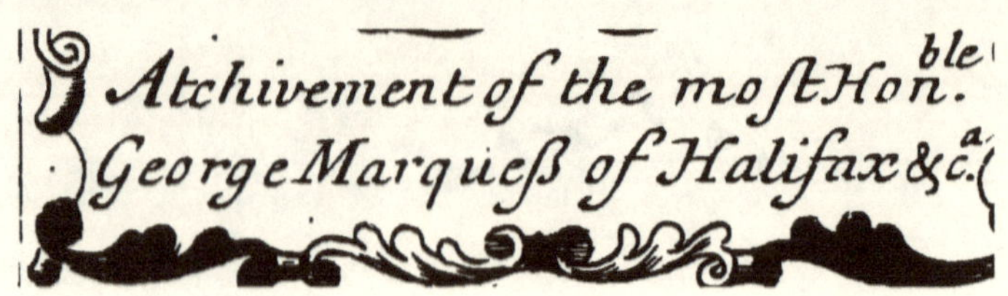

Atchivement of the most Hon.ble
George Marqueß of Halifax &c.a

the abſence of the *King*, or a *Duke* he may have his Clothof Eſtate reaching within a yard of the Ground; and his *Marqui-neſs* may have her Train born by a Knights Lady in her own Houſe, but not in the preſence of a *Dutcheſs*. His eldeſt Son hath the Title of Earl, and his younger Sons are *Lords* Alſo his eldeſt Daughter is a *Counteſs*, and his younger *Ladies* by curteſie.

For the example of the Bearing of a *Marquiſs*. I ſhall incert that of the moſt Honourable *George Savil*, Baron of *Eland*, Viſcount, Earl and Marquiſs of *Hallifax*, Lord *Privy Seal*, and one of the Lords of his Majeſties moſt Honourable *Privy Coun-cel*, &c. who Beareth for his paternal Coat Armour Pearl, on a Bend *Diamond* three *Owls* of the Field. Mantled Ruby, doubled Ermine, and for his Creſt on a *Coronet* and *Helmet* befiting his Lordſhips Degree, on a *Wreath* or *Torce* of his Colours, an *Owl* Pearl, ſupported by two *Talbots* Pearl, gorged about the Necks with *Ducal Crowns* per Pale Pearl and Ruby. And for his Motto in an Eſcrole *BE FAST*.

Marquiſs
of *Halli-fax*.

EARLS

E A R L S.

See Guil-
lim Se-
cond Part
Chapt. 6.

THE word Earl by the *Saxons* was called *Erlig*, or *Ethlin*; by the Ger-
manes *Plsgrave* or *Lantgrave*, and by the
Normans Counts being esteemed compani-
ons for *Kings* and *Princes*; they were Officers of great trust in former times in
England, and have those *Ensigns* of Honour as the *Marquisses* and *Dukes*, viz. a
Chapeau or *Cap* for the *head* with a *Coronet*
of Gold which for distinction is *Pyramidal* pointed and pearled, and between
each *Pyramide* is a *Flower* much shorter
then the *Pyramid*.　Their Body is adorned
with *Robes*, viz. a *Hood*, *Surcoat*, and *Mantle* of *Scarlet* as for a Marquiss, but there
is but three Guards of Ermine Fur on the
Shoulders; they are also begirt with a
Sword and have a Patent delivered them.
Their Titles are the Right Honourable,
and truly Noble Lord, as also most Potent and Noble Lord, out of his Superiours presence he may have a Cloth of
State fringed with *Pendants*, and his Coun-
tess may have her Train born up by an
Esquires Wife.　　　　　　　　　　　For

Atchivement of the Right Honble
George Carle of Berkeley &c.^a

For the Example of the Bearing of an *Earl* I shall make use of the *Atcheivement* of the Right Honourable *George* Earl of *Berkley*.

The Right Honourable *George* Earl of *Berkley*, Viscount *Duresley*, Lord *Berkley*, *Mawbray*, *Segrave* and *Bruce*, and Baron of *Berkley Castle* and one of the Lords of his *Majesties* most Honourable *Privy Councel* Anno Domino 16—— descended frome *Harding* a younger Son of one of the Kings of *Denmark* hat came into *England* with *William* the *Conquerour*. Who Beareth for his Paternal *Coat Armour* Ruby a *Cheveron* between ten Crosses form Pearl, above the same, on a *Coronet* and *Helmet* befitting his *Lordships* quality a *Wreath* of his *Colours*, thereon a *Miter* Ruby charged with his Honours Coat mantled Ruby doubled Ermine, supported by two *Lions* Pearl, the sinister Crowned, and gorged about the neck with a *Collar* and *Chain* reflecting over his back Topaz, and on a Scrole below his Lordships Motto *VIRTUTE NON VI.*

Atchievement of the Earl of Berkley.

VISCOUNTS.

See *Guill.*
Chap. 7.

Viscount (an ancient name of office now in being for such that are *Sheriffs* of Counties) was about the eighteenth of King *Henry* the Sixth made a Degree of *Honour* who conferred the *Title* on *John* Lord *Beaumont* by *Letters Patents*, by which he was Created (as an Earl) having a *Hood, Surcoat,* and *Mantle* with two *Guards* and a half of plain white Fur on his *Shoulders* (whereas other *Degrees* above this are Ermin'd) and hath his *Coronet* and *Chaplet* with a row of *Pearls* close set together on it. They have the Title of Right Honourable and truly Noble, or potent Lord. His *Viscountess* may have her train born up by a woman out of her Superiours presence.

Atchievement of the Lord Viscount VVenman.

For the Example of the Bearing of a Viscount I shall incert the Atchievement of the Right Honourable *Phillip* Viscount *Wenman* of *Tuam* in the County of *Galloway* in *Ireland,* and Baron *Wenman* of *Kilmainham* in the County of *Dublin* in the said Kingdom of *Ireland;* who beareth two Coats quar-

OMNIA
BONIS
Atchivement of the Right Hon.ble
Richard Lord Viscount Wenman &c.

quarterly, first *Ruby* and Saphir a Cross *Patence* Topaz Secondly, a *Fess* between three *Anchors* Topaz; the Third as the Second, the Fourth as the first; supported by two *Greyhounds* Ruby *Collered*, Topaz; Mantled Ruby, doubled Ermine, and for his *Crest* on a *Coronet* and *Helmet* befitting his Lordships D-gree, on a *Wreath* of his Colours a *Cocks Head* erazed Saphir, *Crested* and *Jollaped* Topaz; And for his *Motto* in an *Escrole* O M N I A   B O N A   B O N I S.

The said Dignity of Viscount, and Baron *Wenman* is by Letters Patents, Created on the Honourable Sir *Richard Wenman* of *Caswell* in *Oxfordshire* Baronet to commence after the death of the said *Philip* Lord Viscount *Wenman*.

LORDS

LORDS SPIRITUAL.

EPiscopacy is as ancient as *Christian Religion*, being ordained by the Apostles who took that Office upon them, and commended it to their Successors where they planted the *Gospel*.

They are *Barons* of the Realm by *Writ*, by *Tenure*, and by *Consecration*. They are in *Precedency* next after *Viscounts*, and are placed upon the Kings right hand in *Parliament*. They have the Title of *Lords*, and Right Reverend Fathers in *God*; and their *Sees* by the Piety of former Ages are amply endowed with revenues sufficient to maintain their Dignities. There are two *Arch-Bishops*, viz. *Canterbury*, and *York*, under whom are five and twenty *Suffragan Bishops*, six and twenty *Deans* of Cathredrals and *Collegiate Churches*, sixty *Arch Deacons*, and 544 *Prebendaries*.

The Arch-Bishop of *Canterbury* is *Metropolitan* of *England* hath power to Summon the *Archbishop* of *York*, with the Bishops of his *Province* to a National *Synod*; he takes place of all *Dukes*, and grea

Arch-Bishops, Bishops, Deans.

great *Officers* at *Court* except the Royal Family; his Office is to Crown the King. The *Bishop* of *London* is his *Provincial Dean*, *Winchester* his *Chancellor*, and *Rochester* his *Chaplain*.

The *Arch-bishop* of *York* also hath precedency of all *Dukes* except those of the *Royal Blood* and of all *Great Officers* except the Lord *Chancellor* or Lord *Keeper*; he hath the Honour to Crown the *Queen* and to be her *Chaplain*.

Archbishops have the Title of Grace, and most Reverent Fathers in GOD. They have their *Armorial Ensigns* of *Honour* which is the Coat of their Episcopal See, on the Dexter side impaled with their *Paternal Coat*, and for External Ornaments, there is placed above a Miter, with *Keys Saltierwise*, according to this example.

Charles

TEMPORAL BARONS.

See *Guill.*
Nar. 2d.
Chap. 9.

A Baron is a Dignity next unto a Viscount, and our Law Books makes a difference between *Dukes, Marquisses, Earls,* and *Viscounts,* which are allowed Names of Dignity, and the *Baron*; for they affirm that such a Baron needs not to be named *Lord,* or *Baron* by the *Writ,* but the *Duke, Marquis,* &c. ought to be named by their *Names* and *Dignity.* This Dignity is very ancient, they were first called *Valvasors,* which name the *Saxons* chang'd into *Thanes,* and the *Normans* to *Barons.* And 'tis the received opinion that in those days every Earl had ten Barons under him, every *Baron* ten *Knights fees* holden of him, and those that had four *Knights fees* in *Possession* were usually called to the Degree of a *Baron.*

Three
sorts of
Barons.

There are three sorts Or kinds of Barons. *viz.* by *Tenure,* by *Writ,* and by *Creation* or *Patent.*

1. Barons by *Tenure* or *Prescription* are those that hold any *Honour, Castle,* or *Mannor,* as the head of their *Barony* of
which

which there are two forts *Spiritual* and *Temporal* and thefe are the moft ancient Barons.

2*dly.* *Barons* by *Writ* are thofe to whom a *Writ* of *Summons* in the *Kings* name is di- rected to come to Parliament, *&c.* which kind of Writ is the fame as directed to *Barons* by *Tenure*, as alfo to Barons by *Patent*; but thofe that are not *Barons* by *Tenure* nor *Patent*, and have only fuch *Writs*, after the receipt of fuch a *Writ* and place taken in *Parliament* accordingly ought to enjoy the *Name* and *Dignity* of a *Baron*.

Barons by Writ.

The firft inftitution of them is fuppofed to be in the 49 of *Henry* the *Third*, to fupply the places of the *Rebellious Barons* then engaged againft him in a Civil War.

3*dly.* *Barons* by *Patent* are Created by the *Kings Letters Patents* to them and their Heirs Male lawfully begotten, and this was begun in the Reign of King *Richard* the Second.

Barons by Patent.

Barons have their *Hood* or *Chapeau*, their *Surcoat* and *Mantle* which hath two guards of *white Fur*, on their *Shoulders*: Alfo a *Coronet* with fix *Pearls* placed at equal diftance.

They have the Titles of Right Ho-
Q nourable

nourable, and truly noble Lords, and the *Baroness* may have her train born up by her Page.

For the Example of a Barons Atchievement, I shall incert the Coat Armour of the *Right Honourable Digby* Lord *Gerrard*, Baron of *Gerrards Bromley* in *Staffordshire*, &c. who beareth Pearl a *Saltier* Ruby. for his *Crest* on a *Coronet* and *Helmet* befitting his Lordships degree, on a Wreath of his Colours a *Munky* proper with a *Chain* over his back Topaz, Mantled Ruby, doubled Ermine, supported by two *Lions* Ermine crowned Topaz.

KNIGHTHOOD.

KNIGHTS of the GARTER.

IT was the custom and policy of puissant Princes both ancient and modern to carals men of Heroick Spirits and renown with remarks of Honour, *viz.* precedency of place, honourable *Robes* and

Badges

Guillim.
Part 2.
Chap. 11.

Atchivement of the Right Hon.-ble
Digby Lord Gerard of Bromley &c.

Badges, and additional Titles; amongſt which none ſeems more ancient then that of *Knighthood*, moſt Nations having divers diſtinct orders, ſome *Military*, and ſome *Civil*; but amongſt all orders purely *Military* that of Saint *George* which we call *Knights* of the *Garter* deſervedly hath the preheminence for it's antiquity, glorious inſtitution by that Triumphant King *Edward*, and for the many *Emperours*, *Kings* and *Princes* that have thought themſelves honoured in being admitted into the Fraternity.

It was inſtituted about the year 1350, by the victorious King *Edward* the *Third*. The *Patron* of the order is Saint *George* a man of renown for *Chivalry* and *Chriſtianity* in confirmation whereof he ſuffered Martyrdom in *Aſia*, to whoſe memory many *Temples* and *Monaſteries* were dedicated in the Eaſtern, and afterwards in the Weſtern *Churches*. And the 23*th*. of *April* is aſſigned for his Feaſt.

The number of *Knights* of the *Garter* are not to exceed ſix and twenty, but there is uſually left one or more vacancies for the gratifying a foreign *Prince*, or *Ally*.

The Habit of the order are Robes of

Crimson, and Purple *Velvet Cassocks*, with *Collers* to be worn over them on Feast and Solemn Days, and a Star of *Silver* to be embroidered on the left side of their *Cloaks*, or *Coats*. They are also to wear the Image of Saint *George* on Horseback encountring with the *Dragon* to be made of Diamonds set in Gold, which is to hang on a blue Ribon, and always worn cross their Body or Shoulders, as also a *Garter* on the left Leg Enamelled with Gold, Pearl, and precious Stone with the Motto *HONI SOIT QUI MALY PENSE.* Or instead thereof a *Blew Ribbon,* of all which stately *Robes,* together with the Solemnities at their Instaulation, *&c.* is at large treated of by Mr. *Ashmele.*

The distinction of Honour in their *Shields* is always within a *Garter* according to the examples following, born by the Right Noble *Henry* Duke of *Beaufort* Marquiss and Earl of *Worcester,* Baron *Herbert* of *Chipstow, Raglon* and *Gower,* Lord *President,* and Lord Leiutenant of *Wales,* and *Marshes,* Lord *Leiutenant* of the Counties of *Glocester, Hereford,* and *Monmouth,* and of the City and County of *Bristol,* Lord *Warden* of his Majesties

Atchievement of the Duke of Beaufort.

Forest

Atchivement of his Grace —
Henry Duke of Beaufort &c.ª

of *Dean*, and Conftable of the Caftle of
St. *Briavells*, Knight of the moft noble
Order of the *Garter*, and one of the Lords
of his *Majefties* moft Honourable *Privy
Councel*, &c. who beareth within a *Garter*,
France and *England*, quarterly within a
Border Gobonated Pearl and Saphir. En-
figned with a *Coronet* and *Helmet* befiting
his Graces quality, thereon on a Wreath
of his Colours a *Pureullis* Topaz, mantled
Ruby doubled Ermine, fupported on the
Dexter by a *Panthur* Pearl, fpotted of
all Colours, collored, and chained Topaz, with Flames of Fire iffuing out of
his Mouth and Ears proper. On the finifter fide a *Wivern* emeral'd, gorged a-
bout the Neck with a Crown Ducal, and
Chain reflecting over his back Topaz,
holding in his mouth a dexter hand couped Ruby; and for his Motto in an
Efcrole *MUTARE VEL TI-
MERE SPERNO.*

KNIGHTS BANERETS.

THIS Order of *Knighthood* was in former Times reputed *Barons*, and had the admittance amongst the *Peers* in *Parliament*, in the *Saxon Regiment*, amongst the *French* the Honour was *Hereditary*, but with us now adays for Life only, yet they retain some *Ensigns* of Honour, such as *Supporters*, and have Precedency of all under the *Degree* of a *Baron*. But they must be such *Banerets* as are made under the *Royal Standard displayed*, in time of battle the *King* or *Prince* being present, of this *Order*, there is at present none that I can hear of living.

BARONETS.

THE lowest degree of *Hereditary Honour* is that of a *Baronet*, instituted by King *James*, *Anno* 1611. They are created by *Patent* under the *Great Seal* as the *Nobles*, to them and their Heirs male lawful-

ly

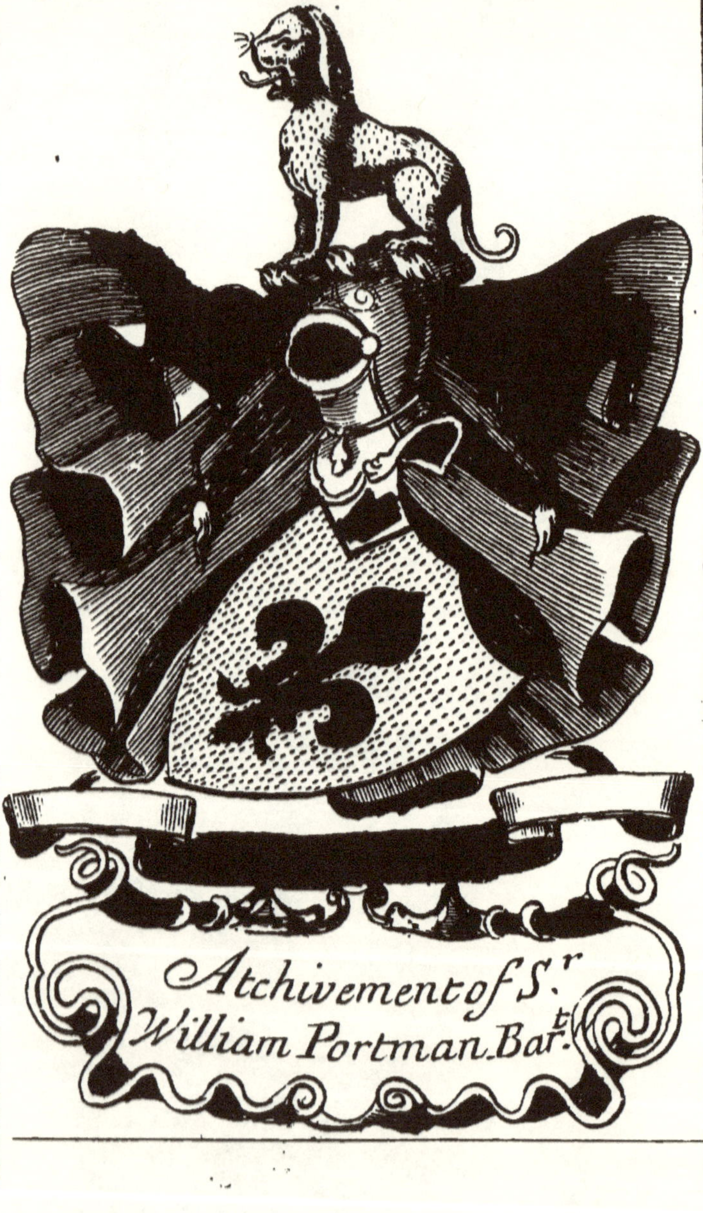

Atchivement of Sr
William Portman. Bart.

ly begotten, without otherwise by a particular Clause: They are styled in all *Writs* and *Commissions Baronets*, with the Addition of *Sir*, and the Title of *Lady* to their *Wives*.

There are also *Baronets* of *Nova-Scotia* for *Scotland*, but these of *England*, as an *Armorial Ensign* of their Honour, bears on a *Canton*, or in an *Escochion* placed in some convenient and perspicuous Place of the *Shield*, the *Arms* of *Ulster*, (viz.) Argent, a sinister hand couped at the wrist, Gules.

For the *Example* of the *Bearing* of a Baronet, *I* shall incert the *Archievement* of Sir *William Portman* of *Orchard* in *Somersetshire* Kt. of the *Bath* and *Baronet*, who beareth for his Paternal Coat Armour Or, a *Flower de lis* Azure on a Canton, the *Arms* of *Ulster* as aforesaid : And for his Crest on a *Helmet*, befitting his Degree, a Wreath of his Colours, thereon a *Talbot Seiant* Or, mantled Gules doubled Argent.

There are some *Baronets* that besides the *Augmentation* of a *hand* as aforesaid by a peculiar Grant doth bear *Supporters*; for an Example I shall make use of the Atchievement of the Honourable Sir *Henry Gord-*

Baronet
Nova scotia.

Sir *William Portman.*

Sir *Henry Geodrick.*

Goodrick of *Ribston-Park* in *York-shire* Kt.
and Bar. His Majesties *Envoy* Extraordinary to the King of *Spain*, *Anno Domini*,
168⅔, who beareth Argent, on a Fess
Gules, between Two *Lyons passant* Gardant, Sable, a Flower de lis Or, between
two *Crescents* Argent: For his *Crest*, on a
Helmet, and *wreath* of his *Colours*, a *Demy-
Lyon* Sable, holding a *Pole Ax* Argent,
Mantled Gules, double Argent, for his
Supporters two *Naked Boys* proper, and for
his *Motto* in an *Escrole FORTIOR LEO-
NE JUSTUS.*

KNIGHTS *of the* BATH.

THESE *Knights* are so called from
Part of the *Ceremonies* at their *Creation*, which is at the *Coronation* of a *King*
or *Queen*, or at the Creation of a Prince
of *VVales*, or of a Duke of the *Blood-Roy-
al*.

This Order saith *Froysard* was instituted *in Anno* 1399. by K. *Henry* the *IV*, but
others say they are of a longer continu-
ance, being then revived after a *Disu-
sage*.

They

Atchivement of the Honoura.ble
Sr Henry Goodrick &ca

They have *Robes* and *Ceremonies* appropriate to them, they wear a *Red Ribbon* crofs their left fhoulder to which a Medal (being the Gift of the *King* or *Prince* that creates them) is affixed.

There is no *Badge* of Honour in their *Arms*, being in all refpects the fame as to external Ornaments with a *Knight Batchelor*.

KNIGHTS BATCHELORS.

KNights *Batchelors* are fuch that are raifed to this *Dignity* for their *Prowefs* and *Merit*, being at firft a *Military Honour*, and beftowed as well for their *Reward*, as to encourage others to Noble *Atchievements*.

They are called *Knights Batchelors*, as *Selden* in page 458. notes from *Buccellarii* fignifying in the declining Empire a *Souldier* or Servant muft be ready for *Military Employment*, to which word *Chevalier* was joyned to denote a Souldier tryed and fit for *Horfe Service*, and by their Honourable *Atchievements* obtained great repute throughout the Chriftian World.

In

In all Foreign-Countreys *Knights* have place according to their being *Knighted*, a Privilege debarred *Noblemen*; for be they never fo Noble and Antient, they are only reputed as *Gentlemen* in Foreign *Countreys,* and cannot demand Place of the youngeft Knight there by *Law* or *Arms*.

The other *Privileges* and *Honours* allowed them in *England* is at large difcourfed in *Guilims Heraldry, Second Part. Chap.* 21.

Atchieve-
ment of
Sir Robert
Dafhwood.

For the Bearing of a *Knight Batchelor, I* fhall incert the *Atchievement* of Sir *Robert Dafhwood.*

He beareth *Argent* on a *Fefs* between a double *Coitize,* Gules, 3 *Griffons* heads Erazed Or, Mantled Gules doubled Argent, and for his Creft, on a Helmet and Wreath of his Colours a *Griffons Head Ermenois* erazed *Gules.* This is the Atchievement of Sir *Robert Dafhwood* of *Norbrook* and *Wickham* in *Oxfordfhire* Kt.

E S Q U I R E S.

ESQUIRE by the *Latin* Word *Armiger* seemeth to take it's Original from Bearing the *Armour* of a *King*, *Duke*, or some great *Warrier*, as we find *Saul* and *Jonathan* to have their *Armour Bearers*; likewise *Troilus* and *Achiles* and *Clytus Alexander* the great in the same Office; so that amongst all *Civil Nations* such Men were in use, and of such reputation in those ancient days, that their *Posterity* were careful to own their *Descent*, and to continue the *Title*, and as in those antient Times, so are these in our days descended (for the most part) of worthy *Ancestors*, that for their warlike Exploits, or for their *merits* and *service* of the *Commonwealth* in times of Peace, had both the Title of *Esquires*, and *Coats* of *Arms* allowed, or bestowed on them, and their *Descendants* as a Reward for the same, of those that bear that Title amongst us are several sorts of *Honours* that precede *Knights*, and such are the Eldest Sons of *Viscounts* and *Barons* and *Noblemens* younger

ger *Sons* of the second rank, are the Se-
lect Esquires of the *Kings* Body, then
Knights Eldest Sons. In a fourth rank
are such as the King together with the
Title, giveth *Arms* or *Creates Esquires* by
Impoſition of a Silver *Coller* or *SS*, or
by Patent *Creamus te Armigerum*; &c.
and that but rarely.

In the firſt place are reckoned all ſuch
Gentlemen as by the *Kings Patent*, under
the *Great* or *Privy Seal* are ſo Intituled by
reaſon of their publick *Offices*, &c. and
ſuch are all *Serjeants* at *Law*, *Juſtices* of
the *Peace*, *Sheriffs* and other *Officers* and
Commanders Military and *Civil*.

Laſtly *Esquires* by Reputation, the
Principal whereof are thoſe that Attend
Knights of the *Bath* at their Creation, then
Barriſters at *Law*, *Mayors* of *Cities*, Offi-
cers of *Courts*, &c.

The better ſort of *Esquires* are ſtiled
Worſhipful.

For the Example of the bearing of an
Esquire, which is the ſame of a Gentleman, I ſhall incert the Atchievement of
William Stych of *Newbury* in the Pariſh of
Barkin in *Essex* Eſquire, who beareth Sable
three *Garbs* Or, Impaled with the Arms
of *Longueville*, viz. Gules a *Fess Dam-*
cetts

Atchivement of
William Stych Esqr

cotte Ermine between six *Cross Croslets Fitche* Argent, in right of his Wife *Margaret Maria*, Daughter of Sir *Thomas Languevile* of *Wolverton* in *Buckinghamshire* Baronet ; and for his Crest on a Helmet and Wreath of his Colours an *Eagle Displayed* Argent, Gorged with a *Coller* Azure, and holding in his *Beak* a *Trefoil slipped* Proper, Mantled Gules doubled Argent, and for his *Motto* in an *Escrole* PRO PATRIA MORI.

GENTLEMEN.

GEntlemen had their beginning either of Blood, *viz.* Such as were born of worthy Parents, or that had done some noble exploit in War whereby they deserved to Bear *Arms* and to be accounted *Gentlemen*, but now a days whosoever studieth the Laws of the *Realm* at any of the Inns of *Court* or *Chancery*, or who is a student at the *Universities*, also he that professeth the liberal *Sciences*, or can live without manual labour, or by his Wealth can live and bear the Port of a *Gentleman*, shall be called Mr. and may

may purchase a Coat of *Arms* to himself and posterity. And the *Saxons* admitted none to the Estate of *Gentry* out of all the *Trades* conversant in Gain, but such, only as encreased their Wealth by honest *Husbandry*, or plentiful *Merchandize* from beyond the *Seas*.

Some others there are that number up nine several sorts of *Gentlemen*. First, those of *Ancestry* which must be *Gentlemen* of *Blood*. Secondly, those of *Blood*, and not of Ancestry, as when he is the second degree descended from the first. Thirdly, *Gentlemen* of *Coat Armour* and not of *Blood*, as when he beareth a device given him by the *Heralds*, and then he and his issue are so stiled to the third descent, who are *Gentlemen* of *Blood*. Fourthly *Gentlemen* of *Coat Armour* and not of blood, as when the King gives them and their Heirs a *Lordship* by vertue thereof they may bear the *Coat Armour* of the old *Lord*, the *Heralds* approving thereof, and provided the said old Lords Family is extinct. Fifthly, a *Christian Soldier* that in the Service of *God* and his *Prince* killeth a *Heathen Gentleman* he shall bear his Arms, and if he hath issue to the third *Degree*, then they are Gentlemen of
blood;

Atchivement of the Right
Noble Frances Stewart Dutcheß
dowager of Richmond &c.ᵃ

blood ; but note that no *Christian Soldier* may bear another *Christians Coat* although vanquished by him in *Battle*, but may bear his Coat, in the finister *Quarter* with the proper Coat of fuch a Gentleman that he killed or put to flight, provided it be done in an *Army Royal.* Sixthly, if the *King* Knight a *Yeoman* he is then adjudged a *Gentleman* of blood. Seventhly, when a *Yeomans* Son is advanced to *Spiritual Dignity* he is then a Gentlman, but not of *Blood*, except he be a Doctor of the Civil *Laws.* Eightly, or fuch that are brought up in a *Cathredral* or *Abbey* there ferving in good office, or fuch as are of near kind to the *Bishop* or *Abbot.* And, Ninthly, fuch as ferve a *Prince* as a *Page* : and afterwards by their diligent and faithful fervice are advanced to higher places although without badge by *Birth* are efteemed Gentlemen.

Thus you fee the *Scale* of *Nobility* both *Major* and *Minor.* In the next place I fhall give you the *Bearing* of a *Woman*, not under *Femme Covert.*

The Right Noble *Frances Steward*, Dutchefs Dowager of *Richmond* and *Lenox* beareth two Coates quarterly ; *Firft*, Saphir ; *Flower de lis* Topaz within a *Border* Ruby

Ruby charged with *Buckles* Topaz. *Secondly*, Topaz a Fess checky Pearl and Ruby within a *Border Engrailed* of the *Third*, the *Third* as the *Second*, and the *Fourth* as the *First*, over all in an *Escocheon* of pretence *Pearl*, a *Saltier* Engrailed between *Four* Cinquefoyls Ruby, Impaled with Pearl, a Bend *Engrailed* Ruby surmounted by a Fess checky Pearl and Saphir, supported by two Wolves proper. It will not be unnecessary to take notice of the principal Parts of *Honour* and *Vertue*, that every Gentleman of what Degree of Honour soever, ought to be endowed with, which are as followeth,

To fear God, and walk after his Commandments, and to his Power to defend *Holy Church*. To love *Honour*, to be loyal and serviceable to his *Prince* and *Country*. To delight in *Military Exercises*, to frequent the *War*, and to prefer Honour before worldly wealth. To be charitable to the distressed, and to support Widows and Orphans. To reverence Majestrates, and those placed in Authority. To cherish *Truth*, *Vertue* and *Honesty*, and to eschew Intemperance, riot, sloth, all dishonest recreations and *Company*. To be courteous, gentle and of an affable Deport-
ment

ment to all men, detesting *Pride*, and *Haughtiness*. To be true and just in word and dealing, and to give no just cause of offence to any man. To be of an open and liberal heart delighting in *Hospitality* and to promote and encourage all publick useful and honourable works, especially such as relate to the advancement of knowledge and learning as the Printing of Books which are lively Monuments Registring to Future Ages an honourable Account of such persons that by whose generosity such undertakings were finished, for what greater satisfaction can it be to any Gentleman to find in Books an Honourable and Commendable Account of his Ancestors which certainly every one should be ambitious of, for Books the *Trumpet* of *Fame* sounds forth their praise not only in their own Country, but throughout the World, and and that to Future Ages. Whereas if no such Remarks were taken of their Families in process of time they will be forgotten, nay probably in that part of their own Countrey where they dwelt, especially upon removals of Families from one Countrey to another which is very accustomary and that for several reasons.

R   PRE-

PRECEDENCY.

PRecendency may be thus obferved. The *King* who is the *Fountain* of Honour. The *Prince* of *England* who is eldeft Son to the King, and is born Duke of *Cornwal*, &c. *Princes* of the *Blood Royal* who are the *Sons*, *Brothers*, *Uncles* and *Nephews* of the King, The Arch-Bifhop of *Canterbury*, the Lord Chancellor, or Lord Keeper of the Great Seal, the Arch-Bifhop of *York*, Lord *Treafurer* of *England*, Lord *Prefident* of the *Privy Councel*, Lord *Privy Seal*, *Dukes*, *Marquiffes*, *Dukes* eldeft Sons, Earls, *Marquiffes* eldeft Sons, Dukes younger Sons, *Vifcounts*, *Earls* eldeft Sons, *Marquiffes* younger Sons, *Bifhops*, *Barons*, *Vifcounts*, eldeft Sons, *Earls* younger Sons, *Barons* eldeft Sons, *Privy Councel* that are not Noblemen, *Judges*, *Vifcounts* younger Sons, *Barons* younger Sons, *Knights* of the *Garter* if not otherwife dignified as is rarely found, *Knights Banerets*, *Baronets*, *Knights* of the *Bath*, *Knights Batchellors*, *Collonels*, *Serjeants* at *Law*, *Mafters* of *Chancery* and Doctors, Efquires, and thofe may be comprehend-

ed

ded under five Heads, 1. Efquires,to the Kings Body, 2dly. The *defcendants* by the Male line from a *Peer* of the Realm. 3dly. The eldeft Sons of Knights of the Garter, Baronets and Knights, 4thly. The two Efquires attending on the Knights of the Bath at their Creation, and 5thly. *officious Efquires* as Juftices of the Peace, Barefters at Law, Leiutenant Collonels, Majors, and Captains, and laftly, Gentlemen of Coat Armour.

An Alphabetical **TABLE** of the **NAMES** of the **NOBILITY** and **GENTRY**, whose **COATS** are made use of for Paterns of **BEARINGS** in this Treatise of **HERALDRY**.

R 3   Boyl

Chol—

The Table

The Table

F I N I S.